MW01611265

ALSO BY FREN THOMPSON

Yours To Know – Poems and rhymes

To Find a Place

DEDICATION

This is the authors' first novel and was inspired by memories of his late mother and father. His father possessed some of the qualities depicted by the main character, Albert.

ACKNOWLEDGMENTS

The author expresses appreciation to his wife Inez and
daughter Lorraine, who both contributed their literary and
editorial skills to the final compilation of this novel.
Without them this work would have been much more
difficult.

"There is a magnet in your heart that will attract true friends. That magnet is unselfishness, thinking of others first; when you learn to live for others, they will live for you."

- Paramahansa Yogananda, Indian monk, yogi, and guru

This is a story about dedicated men and women who strive to enhance the lives of those less fortunate than themselves. By doing so, they make the world a more harmonious place.

1

Olan Noble tapped his foot impatiently as he waited outside his home in Scotland. It was two fifty in the afternoon and the taxi had not yet arrived. He had requested a pick-up time of two thirty and could not believe that the taxi driver was late. He glanced at his watch for the tenth time and sighed with exasperation. This taxi service really sucks, he muttered to himself.

Last night his mother had been inconsolable. She had sobbed as she rested her head on his shoulder.

"I don't want you to go," she had whispered in his ear. "Please, please, don't go."

He had hugged her tightly and gently rubbed her back.

"It will be okay. You know that I have to do this. You can come and visit me soon. Please don't cry anymore," he had pleaded.

His plea had been in vain. His mother had sobbed incessantly. An endless stream of tears had run down her cheeks, and he had felt powerless to stop them. He had finally released her and walked away, making sure to hide the tears in his own eyes. Now the memory of his mothers' tear-stricken face and soft helpless sobs were torturing him. He heard her voice resounding in his head as he waited for the taxi.

Olan angrily wiped away a tear. He hated being delayed now that it was finally time to leave Scotland. He just wanted to board the ship and be on his way to Trombago. He hoped that he would feel better once he got onboard.

A seagull squawked as it flew by and it reminded him of days he had spent on the beach with his mother. Back then he had watched as seagulls sunk their beaks into the sea, retrieved fishes, and then flew away. They always squawked loudly and fluttered their wings wildly as they foraged for food. Olan remembered running with reckless abandon towards those seagulls on the boardwalk, hoping to get to them before they flew away. On the rare occasions when he got to the boardwalk in time, he would wave his arms and scream with all his might. Then the seagulls would fly away and he would squeal with delight to see their wings above him at close range. Those days seemed so near, and yet they were long gone. Though they would never return, he would always have those everlasting memories.

Olan had many cherished childhood memories. He was his mothers' only son, and the youngest of her four children. He and his mother had always shared a close and loving relationship. She had schooled him until he was five years old when he entered public school, and then helped him with all his schoolwork. She taught him how to cook and clean, and how to be brave, strong and persistent. He would miss her very much. He could only hope that the love they had for each other would keep them both strong.

Olan glanced at his watch again. It was three o'clock. He shifted his sunglasses and peered down the street. Finally, he saw the taxi approaching.

2

Greff Ives stood at the end of the pier looking across the wide expanse of the sea. His tie fluttered in the wind and, because of the wind, his eyes were teary. He pulled a handkerchief from his pocket and wiped them gently.

"When do you actually begin working?" Fleet asked him.

"One week after I get there. That is supposedly enough time to assess and finalize the plans for the estate," Greff replied.

"Have you been given the strategic plans to review ahead of time?" Fleet asked.

"No," Greff replied, "but I received the mission and vision statement. That is a good enough start."

Fleet was Greffs' only brother. He was older than Greff and was always ready to provide him with help and advice whenever he needed it. He was proud of Greffs' achievements and strongly supported his decision to migrate to Trombago to organize and manage The Trifecta Sugar Cane and Agriculture Estate. Greff was the physical type. He was muscular and strong and adept at organizing and promoting, as well as at implementing procedures and processes.

The brothers gazed across the ocean, enjoying the silence between them and cherishing their brotherly bond. The air was fresh and clean, the afternoon sunny and bright, and the sea was a deep dark blue. Taxis and cars arrived at the dock within minutes of each other, and passengers of all ages, sizes, and ethnicities retrieved their luggage and made their way up the ships' gangplank. Greff was in no hurry to board the ship. He was enjoying the final moments with his brother in the country of his birth. It would be many months before he saw land, and his brother, again.

Suddenly the ships' horn blared.

"Well, this is it!" Greff exclaimed.

"Yes. Your journey is about to begin," Fleet replied. "I wish you God's speed my brother. I also wish you much success and happiness. Make sure to write as soon as you arrive and get settled."

"Thanks. Be safe and well. I'll write soon," Greff replied.

Greff strolled up the gangplank. He had a swagger and an air of confidence. He was looking forward to his new job and new life in Trombago. He hummed a merry tune as he climbed on board the ship.

The ship was huge and there were passengers everywhere. The air was filled with a mixture of sadness, gladness, and anticipation as passengers chatted with each other or waved to their loved ones on the shore. The rhythmic lashing of the waves against the ship seemed like a lullaby intended to assuage emotions and provide a sense of certainty about the coming expedition.

Despite the hustle and bustle Greff found his cabin easily and after storing his luggage, he headed for the bar.

3

Olan opened the door of the taxi before it came to a complete stop at the dock. He was eager to get on board the ship and settle down for the long voyage. A gentle breeze caressed his face as he paid the taxi driver and collected his luggage from the car trunk. He wondered how comparable this breeze was to the breeze from the Caribbean Sea. Taking a deep breath, he ascended the gangplank.

Deep within the hull of the ship the captain and his supporting officers manned their stations. A voice came through the loudspeakers.

"Good afternoon, this is your captain speaking. Welcome aboard the Maidenstrum. We will set sail in fifteen minutes."

Olan deftly avoided a scurrying child. It seemed as though children were everywhere. The giggling, frolicking, energetic children were in direct contrast to the serious, cautious adults who tended luggage or gazed longingly at their loved ones who were at the shore.

Olans' cabin was on the lower deck. As he climbed down the stairs the memory of his mother returned and he sighed. He decided that he would have her visit him very soon.

Once inside his cabin Olan stored his luggage and pulled a novel from his briefcase. He was looking forward to spending most of the voyage reading. Before settling down to read however, he walked over to the window and looked out. The sea was breathtaking. Although it seemed never-ending it also seemed to, at the same time, dissolve into nothingness. He took a deep breath, enjoying the ebb and flow of the waves and feeling comforted by their rhythmic motion.

The captains' voice broke into his reverie.

"We are now ready to sail. Once more, welcome aboard. We will keep you posted as needed throughout our journey."

Olan smiled and opened his novel. Soon he was engrossed in a murder mystery that took his mind away from his mother and the long journey ahead.

4

Glen Mariposa had been estate supervisor for three years. He ran the estate as best as he could with a meager staff of twelve men. Although sugar cane was the main crop cultivated on the estate, there were banana and orange orchards as well as corn and potato fields. The estate produced enough harvest to keep afloat, but there was a need for strong planning and oversight to maximize yearly output and ensure increased output from year to year.

"Massa Glen! Massa Glen!" Primrose shouted. She sounded out of breath.

Glen opened the door of the tool shed.

"Yes Primrose," he replied.

"De plough wheel bruk off!" Primrose exclaimed.

Glen quickly went with Primrose to the field. When he got there, he groaned. The right wheel of the plough had cracked in two places. It had then separated from the cart. There was nothing Glen could do but wrap up ploughing in that field for the day. He would have to go into the town and purchase a replacement wheel. He instructed the field workers to help the workers in the adjacent field. Even though production in the current field would cease for the day he drew consolation from the fact that, with additional workers, the output in the other field would therefore surpass the days' target.

Glen prepared to go into town. He had plenty of time to get there, purchase a new plough wheel at the farm equipment store as well as food supplies at the haberdashery, then spend some time with Walt before heading to the port. Walt was Glens' only sibling. He attended college in the town and worked at the largest haberdashery there. He lived in a tiny room near to the college and spent most of his time in the town.

Glens' mother, fondly known as Miss Etta, provided Glen with three canteens of water to take with him. It had been sweltering hot all day, and the water would provide hydration during the trip. Miss Etta was in charge of the household at the estate. She maintained strong supervision over the household help and ensured that the house was spotless at all times. He loved her dearly and was extremely protective of her, especially after his father passed away two years ago.

"Give this package to Walt," she said, "and give him my love."

It was her special and very popular pound cake. She knew that Walt loved it. Glen smiled. Miss Etta was a kind, considerate soul.

5

The Maidenstrum had been sailing for twelve weeks and was now nearing the port in Trombago. Olan leaned against the railing on the eastern side of the ship and yawned. The voyage had been uneventful. The weather had been good throughout the journey and the amenities on board had been satisfactory. He had particularly enjoyed the nightly entertainment provided by the reggae band. He yawned again and stretched. He felt comforted by the warm and gentle sea breeze.

With a sigh of contentment, Olan continued his stroll alongside the railing. He enjoyed being on deck at this time of the day. Almost all of the passengers were in the dining area either eating, or just chatting after eating the big meal provided for lunch. Olan preferred to stroll on deck after eating. It was about two o'clock and he knew that he should return to his cabin and get his stuff sorted for arrival. However, he was enjoying his time on deck and felt reluctant to do that now. His journey had been one of rest and relaxation. The mere thought of sorting and packing his belongings just seemed like work.

A few feet ahead of him a young man was leaning against the railing with his girlfriend snuggled in his arms. They did not notice as he approached. They were absorbed in a deep kiss. Olan smiled as he passed by them. At that moment the captains' voice came through the loudspeaker.

"We are nearing the port of Trombago," he said. "We estimate arrival in three hours. The temperature on the island is ninety-two degrees. We will keep you updated as we get closer to the dock."

With a jolt Olan realized that he would actually be working in Trombago within twenty-four hours. This realization energized him. He was looking forward to it.

6

Glen donned his hat and, picking up the package his mother had prepared, headed for the door. The ship was expected to dock in a little over two hours.

Everything was ready. Two bedrooms on the eastern side of the house had been prepared for Olan and Greff. The bathrooms had been sanitized and stocked with fresh towels, and his mother was now supervising the preparation of the welcome meal.

Glen wondered what the new managers would be like. Would they be strict or lenient? Would they make drastic changes? How would they adjust to the climate, to the food, to the culture? How tolerant would they be of the mosquitoes and lizards? What sort of schedule would they establish? His mind considered these and more as he drove to the farm equipment store.

Taking a sip of water from one of the canteens his mother had provided, Glen nodded his head with determination. No matter what, I will cooperate and help them to adjust; I will share all the information and advice I have about running the estate; as it stands now I have a good job and my mother is secure in the house; I will not do anything to jeopardize my mothers' security, he decided.

Glen drove slowly along the busy streets in the town. Many small cars and trucks loaded with dry goods and produce were being driven along the main road, and some parked vehicles were being loaded or unloaded at the curbside. Some people milled about carrying baskets and bags and shouting greetings to each other, while others stood idly on the sidewalk chatting the time away. The town was a busy place.

Soon Glen pulled up outside the farm equipment store.

In less than thirty minutes he purchased a new plough wheel and was on his way to the haberdashery to purchase food supplies and spend some time with Walt.

"Hey there Glen," Walt said, smiling at Glen as he entered the store.

"Hi Walt. How you been man?" Glen asked.

Glen and Walt hugged.

"I've been good. I've been taking mid-term exams. I have a lot of studying to do, but soon I'll be done with all the exams," Walt replied.

"Good my brother. Keep at it. Success will come if you persevere."

Glen smiled and extended the package with the pound cake.

"Guess what I have here?" he asked.

"Oh, did mamma bake again?" Walt said with a chuckle.

"Yes, she did," Glen replied. "She also sent her love."

"Bless her," said Walt, and chuckled again. "Tell her that I said thanks and that I sent my love. How is she doing?"

"She's well. As you know, she keeps busy and loves being in charge of the household," Glen replied. "It seems quiet in the store today. What time will you take your break?"

"It was very busy in the mid-morning hours," Walt replied. "I like working here. I'll take my break in another fifteen minutes."

"Good. I'll gather the things I need and then we can chat outside for a little while," Glen said.

Soon Glen and Walt sat outside the store and caught up on current circumstances in their lives.

"The new managers of the Estate are arriving today," Glen revealed. "Once I leave here, I will be going to the port to pick them up."

"Wow. That's news. I hope that they will like being in Trombago, and that they will be fair-minded and successful," Walt said.

The brothers talked some more while Walt enjoyed his

lunch and the cake that Miss Etta had made. Soon a customer walked into the store.

"Well, time for me to go back to work," said Walt.

Glen hugged Walt.

"See you soon again my brother. Be well," he said.

"Take care. Tell mamma that I will come to see her next weekend," Walt replied.

Glen arrived at the port just as the Maidenstrum pulled into the dock. There were several vehicles already waiting there. He sat inside his car, marveling at how big the ship was. He wondered if he would ever travel on one. He shook his head and chuckled. Fat chance, he thought. He knew that it was expensive to travel, and he also knew that deep down he did not want to travel anywhere outside of Trombago. Maybe one day I could go on board just to assuage my curiosity about the ship, he thought.

Soon the passengers began to disembark. Glen retrieved his placard from the back of the car and held it in front of him so that Olan and Greff would know that he had come to pick them up. The car had been washed and the interior cleaned just before he left the estate. He was sure that Olan and Greff would be comfortable.

Trombago was known for its long days. At six o'clock in the evening the sun still shone brightly in the sky. It was the perfect day for Olan and Greff to arrive. It had not rained for three days, and rain was not expected any time soon.

Suddenly a taxi driver began blowing his horn at a group of people crossing the street. He seemed impatient and angry. Hurriedly the group of people got out of his way. Glen mentally patted himself on the shoulder for deciding to pick up Olan and Greff. It would really be a shame if they experienced the bad temper of a taxi driver immediately on their arrival, he thought.

"Good afternoon," Olan said, walking up to Glen with his arm extended. "I'm Olan Noble."

"Pleased to meet you. I'm Glen." He shook Olans' hand.

"Welcome to Trombago. How was your journey?"

"It was good. Nothing eventful happened. It is a good vessel to travel on," Olan replied.

"I'm glad to hear that," Glen said. "Once Massa Greff comes, I'll put all the luggage into the car."

Greff walked up while Glen and Olan were exchanging pleasantries.

"You must be Glen," said Greff, with a smile.

"Yes. Welcome to Trombago Massa Greff," Glen replied, with his arm extended. "Did you have a good trip?"

"I did indeed. Thanks for asking," Greff replied. He looked over at Olan. "You must be Olan," he said to him.

"Yes. Good to meet you Greff."

Both men shook hands.

While Olan and Greff climbed into the car, Glen loaded their luggage and soon the men were on their way to the estate. Glen handed them individual canteens of water and turned the air conditioning to full blast. The six o'clock news was being aired on the car radio and the men listened in silence to the latest happenings on the island.

When they arrived at the estate it was almost eight o'clock and the sun had positioned itself a notch above the horizon. The sky had an iridescent orange glow and hues of yellow and orange surrounded the clouds.

"Wow. This is beautiful!" exclaimed Olan.

"It is indeed," Greff remarked.

"We are just in time to watch the sunset," Glen said.

The men got out of the car and Olan and Greff looked around. The land was immaculate. The serenity was palpable.

"I like this," said Greff, nodding his head vigorously.

"My new home away from home," Olan said quietly, as though he was having a conversation with himself.

While Glen pulled the luggage from the car, the sun cast its final brilliant glow and slid below the horizon.

"Let's go inside," Glen said.

Glen walked Olan and Greff to their rooms. Along the way he pointed out the dining and living room areas as well as the door to the kitchen.

"I will go and get the rest of your luggage and leave them outside your rooms. Then I will check back with you in about thirty minutes to walk with you to the dining room. My mother is looking forward to meeting you," Glen said.

Miss Etta was taking a cake out of the oven when Glen walked into the kitchen.

"They're here," Glen said to her. "They'll be coming down for dinner soon. I'll go and freshen up now."

"Alright," Miss Etta replied. "Everything is ready."

Thirty minutes was sufficient time for Olan and Greff to unpack and enjoy a refreshing shower.

"Massa Greff, Massa Olan, meet my mother Miss Etta.

Mamma, this is Massa Greff and this is Massa Olan," Glen said.

"Welcome to Trifecta Massa Greff, Massa Olan," Miss Etta said with a smile.

"Thank you, Miss Etta," Greff replied.

"Happy to be here," Olan replied.

Miss Etta had prepared rice and peas, brown-stewed chicken, and callaloo with fresh red tomatoes. Olan and Greff had never eaten Caribbean food before and did not know what to expect.

"Oh, this looks delicious," Olan commented, and sat down at the table.

"It smells so good," Greff added.

Miss Etta smiled. She loved compliments about her cooking. She loved when people enjoyed a meal she prepared and when they wanted more of it. Without knowing this about Miss Etta, Olan and Greff spared no words of praise. They both enjoyed the meal, as well as the fresh warm ginger cake that Miss Etta had baked for dessert.

"Massa Greff, did you see the big envelope in your room?" Glen asked.

"Yes, I did," Greff replied. "It contains the official strategic plan. By the end of this coming week I will define the workplan and milestones necessary to accomplish the plan."

"This estate covers thirty acres. A little less than one third of it is cultivated. We cultivate sugar cane, bananas, oranges, corn and potatoes. The land is pretty fertile, and we get a good combination of rainy and dry weather to nurture the plants and trees. Our harvest has been good over the years," Glen revealed.

"I understand that there may be a need to reassess staffing and the troughs that are currently in place," Greff said.

"Let's take care of setting up our personal affairs over the next day or so," Olan said. We can get together on Wednesday to start finalizing our action plan."

8

Lirchpin Bank, located in the heart of downtown Trombago, was established in 1902 and reputed to be Trombagos' top bank. Despite the subsequent establishment of three additional banks in Trombago, Lirchpin Bank holds the largest share of a cross-section of the market and is the preferred bank for the rich and prosperous. The bank is housed in a two-story building, with banking operations taking place on both floors. Being the only two-story building in Trombago, the Lirchpin Bank building is a landmark.

Olan arrived there shortly after it opened and was surprised to see quite a number of people waiting on the tellers' line. There were only three people waiting in the business section, however. He signed the waiting list and sat in one of the vacant seats. He was grateful to be inside an air-conditioned building.

The tellers' line was moving slowly, and more people were coming into the bank at a steady rate. Olan recalled his banking experiences in Scotland and found himself comparing those experiences to his present circumstances. He decided that his expectations were unrealistic. He reminded himself that Trombago is a third world country and operated at a slower pace in just about every way. He wasn't in a hurry anyway.

Soon he sat with bank manager, Alicia Brant, and opened business and personal accounts.

"It was a pleasure serving you Mister Noble. If you have any questions, please don't hesitate to give me a call," said Alicia, as she handed Olan starter checks and account disclosures.

"Thank you, Miss Brant. Have a good day," Olan replied.

Warm air greeted Olan when he exited the bank. It was a soothing warmth though. It reminded him of the warmth of his mothers' kitchen after the oven had just been turned off and the smell of freshly baked bread lingered in the air. He hoped that his mother was doing well and that she was carrying out her activities of daily living with normal aplomb. He smiled and said a prayer, thanking God for her and seeking Gods' continued protection, care and blessings for her.

Olan decided to take a stroll through the town before heading back to the estate. As he walked he noticed peddlers sitting on low stools by the roadside, with a variety of vegetables, fruits, herbs and ground provisions displayed on low tables or on canvas spread over the sidewalk. In order to attract customers, the peddlers were shouting the prices at which their produce were being sold. People carrying bags gathered around the peddlers and either made purchases or argued about prices and quality. In some areas garbage and rotten produce had settled in grooves along the sidewalk, and insects and a couple of stray dogs hovered over them. Olan walked at a slow steady pace, absorbing the atmosphere and marveling at the quality of life. He then decided to stroll into the marketplace.

There are several stores inside the marketplace, operated by incorporated business entities. In addition street peddlers set up temporary structures, with items for sale, outside the stores. The marketplace is the busiest place in the town, especially during the late afternoon hours.

At this time in the morning much of the walking space inside the marketplace is taken up with carts pulled by donkeys. Some of them contain vegetables and fruits of all kinds including mangoes, bananas, oranges, callaloo, pumpkin, and tomatoes. Others contain clothing, shoes and household items. Some items are sealed in plastic, others wrapped in brown paper, and still others wrapped in newspaper.

Some peddlers were scampering back and forth,

unloading their goods from the carts, intent on setting up their produce quickly in order to maximize their days' sales. These peddlers were the latecomers. Other peddlers had already unloaded their goods and were either busy making a sale or shouting at passing customers in an effort to make a sale.

"Nice Massa! Nice Massa! Buy sumtin' 'ere! Come! Come! Buy sumtin' 'ere!'"

Olan looked over his shoulder to see a strong middle-aged woman presiding over a large display of bananas, oranges, apples, pumpkin and papaya. He smiled at her as she beckoned to him.

"No, no. Not today," he replied.

You have to be a good hawker to be successful in the marketplace. It is the only way to attract customers and maximize your daily sales. Competition is strong because there are several vendors selling the same item. Since the prices of the items are not fixed, both the vendors and the buyers tend to bargain.

"… a wretch like me. I once was lost, but now I'm found; was blind but now I see. Oh praise da Lord. I once was lost… Hey Massa! Massa!"

Olan looked to his left and saw a thin bald-headed man beckoning to him. He had a set of books displayed on a table, with a burning white candle located in the center of the table.

"Mighty is da Lord, and greatly to be praised. Massa, I see a life a joy and peace fah yuh," the man said, as Olan approached him. He smiled a toothless smile.

"Yuh embark now on a new journey and it will be a happy one. Bless. Bless. Take a look. Take a look," the man said, pointing to the books on his table.

Olan glanced down and saw a collection of books about religion. He picked up one entitled The Religious Dystopia.

"Yes. Yes," the man said, while nodding his head. "Dat is di book fah yuh."

Olan thumbed through the pages.

"Fifty shilling Massa," the man said, extending his open palm.

Abstractedly Olan reached into his pocket and then, putting the book under his arm, retrieved fifty shillings. He handed the money to the man.

"Tank yuh Massa. Tank yuh."

The man smiled his toothless smile again, and Olan somehow felt that he would never forget it.

Continuing his stroll through the marketplace, Olan began to focus on the stores. Most of them were selling a hodge-podge of everything, excluding perishable food items. Other stores were selling only jewelry or clothing, and still others were ready-made garment shops with on-site tailors or/and seamstresses.

Soon Olan made his way to his car and headed back to the estate.

9

During the two years since they arrived on the island, Olan and Greff made a positive impression on their employer, plantation workers and the Trombagonian citizens they interacted with. Now, at the two-year mark, the Trifecta estate was fully cultivated and the staff had doubled in size. Both Olan and Greff had grown to love living in Trombago and had decided to make the island their permanent home. Last year they had returned to Scotland to visit their families and had shared their experiences on, and love of, Trombago with them. They were assured that their families were well and had adjusted to life without them, and so they felt a sense of well-being in their decision to make Trombago their permanent home.

Olan and Greff acquired land adjacent to each other and built neighboring homes. They developed strong social connections with neighbors, farm workers and the community at large. On major holidays they took vacation time and spent a couple days at the Himda Resort – a resort with picturesque landscaping and a breathtaking view of the ocean. The Himda Resort was one of their favorite places on the island and had been instrumental in their decision to make Trombago their home. This resort, and the fact that their love lives had begun to blossom.

Olan had fallen in love with Alicia Brant, the Lirchpin Bank manager. Alicia was a well-educated woman with a flair for finance and dedication to her job. Given these facts and Olans' background in accounting and finance, he was sure that she was his match. Besides, she was slender and shapely, with smooth brown skin, and had big warm eyes and a smile to die for. She spoke with only a slight accent, having been educated at the best schools on the island. The more Olan visited the bank, the harder it was for him to take his mind off her. But he was shy.

Finally Olan mustered enough courage to ask Alicia out to dinner.

"I hope it's not out of place to ask you out to dinner," he said.

Alicia immediately detected Olans' shyness.

"I hope it's not out of place to say yes," she replied.

They both laughed loudly and heartily, oblivious to stares from Alicias' coworkers and the bank customers. Dinner was set for that Friday at the Himda Resort.

Olan left the bank that day with a pep in his step and a smile on his face. His smile remained on his drive home and resurfaced throughout each of the following days until Friday night finally came.

10

T hey were seated at a window table in the restaurant at the Himda Resort. It was the perfect table for them to enjoy the ocean view.

"Good evening sir, madam. May I offer you cocktails?" their waiter said politely.

"Good evening. May I have a bottle of your very best wine?" Olan asked.

"Yes sir," the waiter replied.

Olan became silent. Alicia detected his nervousness and broke the ice.

"Do you come here often?" she asked.

"Not very often. Have you ever been here before?" Olan asked.

"No," Alicia responded. "I am so glad to be here now though. The view is breathtaking."

Soon the waiter returned and poured two glasses of wine. Olan picked up his glass and extended it toward Alicia.

"Here's to the beginning of a wonderful relationship," he said.

Alicia noticed that there was a tremor in Olan's hand. She was touched by his humility. She extended her glass to his and smiled.

"Is this your first date since coming to this country?" she asked.

Olan took a sip of wine.

"It is, and I do hope it is not going to be the last for us," he replied.

Alicia sensed his sincerity and hoped that as he drank more wine his confidence would rise.

Then Olan pointed to the menu.

"I recommend this dish for you," he said.

It was a meal of de-boned lobster cooked in sweet and

sour sauce and topped with thinly sliced carrots and pineapple. It was served with brown rice. This was his favorite meal on the menu. He chose a platter of diced chicken breast and shrimp cooked in young rice for himself.

They soon realized that both dishes went well with their wine.

"This lobster is delicious!" Alicia exclaimed, politely declining a second serving of the wine.

"I'm glad you like it," Olan replied. "Thank you for accepting my invitation. I look forward to doing this again."

"Thank you for inviting me," Alicia replied. "It's not often that I get to socialize because I am so busy at work that I am usually too tired to do so. I must admit that this has been an extraordinarily relaxing evening."

On their way out of the restaurant, Olan met Greff on his way in. After greeting him, Olan introduced him to Alicia.

"I'm so pleased to meet you ma'am," Greff said to Alicia.

Although he was surprised to see Olan and Alicia together, Greff didn't show it. He knew of Olans' love for Alicia but did not know that they had arranged a date.

"I'll have to call for an appointment to see you from now on," Greff said to Olan, with a broad grin on his face.

"It seems so," Olan replied, looking at Alicia.

Olan and Alicia bid Greff goodnight and headed for the car.

"Are you and Greff close friends?" Alicia asked.

"He is more than a friend to me; more like a brother I never had. Since we met here in Trombago we have developed a bond that could only be considered brotherly. I am the only son my parents have. I have three sisters and I am the baby of the family," Olan replied with a smile. "Greff and I were strangers until we met here in this country. I was given the job to oversee and control the finances of The Trifecta Sugar Cane and Agriculture Estate while Greff was assigned to organize, develop and promote the estate. I could never have asked for a better friend or brother. And now that I've met you, my fortunes could never be more blessed."

When they arrived at Alicias' home, Olan opened the gate from the street and held her hand while they strolled along the pathway toward her front door. As they neared the porch, they heard a chuckle and then a faint laugh. They soon realized that Alicias' father, mother and sister were sitting on the porch.

"We waited up for you," her father said, rising from his chair to brighten the dim porch light.

Olan hesitated as Alicia continued toward the porch.

"Come," she said to him.

Olan took a few steps forward.

"Mom, dad, this is Olan. He recently moved here to Trombago and is the financial overseer for the Trifecta estate," Alicia said.

"Pleased to meet you ma'am, sir," Olan said.

Alicia then introduced her sister Joyce.

"Hi Joyce," Olan said.

"I detect a Scottish accent in your speech," Alicias' father remarked.

"Yes sir. I am from near the Cliffs of Dover," Olan replied.

"I am familiar with Dover. I was actually born in England," said Alicias' father. "I came to Trombago in my late teens. I don't think I'll ever live anywhere else. If we can help your transition to island life in any way, please let me know."

"I think you already have. You have a wonderful family," Olan replied.

Alicia looked over at Olan and smiled.

"And so, I must go. I have much to do in the morning," said Olan.

Alicia walked back to the gate with Olan while Joyce trailed behind them. At the gate Olan held Alicias' hand and kissed it gently. Joyce chuckled.

"Now I know where the chuckle we heard earlier came from," Olan said with a smile. "Good night Alicia. And good night to you Joyce."

"Good night," said Alicia and Joyce in unison.

Before falling asleep that night, Olan thought about his date with Alicia and wondered what she thought of him, whether her parents approved, and whether she would go out with him again. He wondered if she was thinking of him that very minute.

The following morning Olan was eager to meet with Greff.

"Did you kiss on your first date?" Greff asked him.

"No, I didn't. Her little sister was in the way," Olan replied. "I also met her parents last night."

Greffs' eyes lit up.

"You did?" he asked.

"They were all waiting up for her," Olan responded. "Her father was born in England."

"Did he interrogate you?" Greff asked.

"Not really," Olan replied. "Just some minor questions; open-ended questions."

Olan sighed and then smiled.

"I can't wait to see her again," he said.

"Go get her, you lion," Greff responded with a laugh.

11

G reff had met Myrna Bovell at a physical fitness lecture at the Himda Resort. She was a school principal and fitness instructor, and she was well loved by school staff, parents and students.

Myrna was the studious type who continuously advanced in knowledge through reading and research. She possessed both a Bachelors' and a Masters' degree, as well as a PhD. Her father was born in Trombago of English parentage and her mother was a native Trombagonian. Myrnas' mother had died in a car accident several years earlier, but fortunately she had lived to see Myrnas' many accomplishments.

Over the years Myrnas' father had lost much of his enthusiasm for life as he continued to grieve over the death of his wife. Myrna was determined to prevent him from giving up on himself. One night after dinner her entire family was sitting in the living room having random discussions.

"What is the greatest need in the island right now?" Myrna asked.

Her bother thought long and hard.

"More homes," he replied.

Her sister chimed in.

"More stores," she said.

After a long silence her fathers' face lit up in the energetic and excited way they all knew and loved.

"More transportation," he said.

A few months later Myrnas' father rolled out a fleet of buses that ran from town to town on the island. The fleet proved to be a sound financial investment. In addition, Myrnas' father was fulfilled by the knowledge that both commuters and the economy benefited tremendously from the bus service. People could now get to and from work, and to various appointments, without being late. Many people no longer had to endure long walks to get to and from their destinations. The transportation business also had a positive impact on Trombagos' GDP and generated significant tax revenue. As a result, Myrnas' father developed a plan to expand the parking garage and increase the fleet within two years.

Greff was fascinated by Myrnas' family history. He loved her humble spirit and her brilliant mind. They would spend many hours walking through the gardens at the Himda Resort, enjoying the crisp clean air, brilliant blue skies, and warm ocean breeze. It was during one of these walks that Greff proposed to Myrna. She said yes with a shy smile.

Later that day Greff told Olan the news.

"Myrna and I are engaged!" he exclaimed.

"Congratulations my man! Did you set a date yet?" Olan replied.

"Yes. We plan the big day for next year, on April twenty-second," Greff said.

"That is good news. But guess what? Alicia and I just set our wedding date. It's this year. Four months from now!" Olan said with a smile.

"What? Awesome! Congratulations! Wow you have a lot to get done before then. Let me know if I can help with anything," Greff responded.

12

On a bright sunny November afternoon Olan and Alicia exchanged marriage vows. The small church was filled with family and friends. Olans' mother and three sisters had travelled from Scotland to be there, and they sat in the front pew.

Olan watched as his beautiful bride walked down the aisle to meet him. As he watched her, he knew that he would always remember her beautiful smile and sparkling eyes. He also knew that he would remember the kiss they would exchange at the altar. But Olan figured that everything else about his wedding day would be a blur, and that that would be okay.

When Olan and Alicia exited the church, they were greeted with loud cheers and showered with rice. Laughing happily, and waving to their guests, they were driven away to the Himda Resort where they were photographed amongst rainbow-colored flowers and shrubs adorned with festive ribbons and sashes. The wedding reception at the Himda Resort was a memorable evening of good food, fine wine and liquor, exotic desserts, laughter, and dancing.

The months flew by quickly. On April twenty-second Greff and Myrna became husband and wife. The church ceremony was elaborate and well attended. Greffs' mother and brother had arrived just in time to attend the ceremony. Olan served as best man and did his part to calm Greffs' nerves while he waited for Myrna to arrive.

Greff was not the only emotional person waiting for Myrnas' arrival. While the organist played a selection of songs by Handel and Brahms, Olan noticed Greffs' mother wiping tears from her eyes. He realized that she was just as proud of, and happy for, Greff as his own mother had been for him.

Myrna smiled with complete confidence as she walked down the aisle. She was a beautiful bride. Her white wedding dress was adorned with pearls and sequins. Her headdress had a long trail that ran down her back and stopped inches away from the end of the trail of her dress. It was also adorned with pearls and sequins. The flowers in her bouquet perfectly matched the white irises and purple tulips arranged throughout the church.

It was a memorable church wedding. Their wedding reception was also held at the Himda Resort, with all the pomp and circumstance worthy of a king and queen.

13

In the following years Olan and Alicia met with Greff and Myrna every week to enjoy fun times together. The four of them shared many things in common. In fact, Myrna and Alicia soon realized that they had attended the same college and taken some courses together. They had however pursued different majors and lost contact with each other. Both women felt a solid connection to each other because of their backgrounds and upbringing.

Their favorite meeting place was the Himda Resort. On Friday nights a pianist played romantic songs at dinnertime. They were enjoying dinner there one Friday night when the pianist began playing When You're Smiling.

"I love that song!" Jean exclaimed.

"Me too!" said Myrna.

"We have some romantic wives, eh Olan?" Greff remarked with a laugh.

"Indeed we do," Olan replied, and laughed.

"Guess what?" Myrna blurted. "Greff and I are expecting our first baby in about seven months! I'm so excited!"

"Wow. That is great news! But, you want to know something? Olan and I are also going to have a baby!" Alicia exclaimed.

Myrna and Jean hugged.

Greff grabbed Olans' hand.

"Congratulations my bother!" he said.

Olan grinned.

"Congratulations to you too!" Olan replied.

Both Greff and Olan were hoping to have boys, while the two women did not have any preference.

"Let's toast! To happy healthy babies!" Greff shouted.

The men knocked their wine glasses against their wives'

juice glasses.

After dinner the couples danced on the terrace to piano-played love songs while the full moon cast a brilliant romantic glow over them.

14

O lan sat patiently in the waiting room at the hospital. He was looking forward to the birth of his first child. He thumbed through a magazine, munched on potato chips, and hummed a merry tune.

"It's a boy!" the nurse exclaimed on entering the waiting room. Olan jumped up from his chair. There was a big smile on his face.

"Can I go in now?" he asked.

"Yes. Yes, indeed. Follow me," the nurse replied.

When Olan opened the door to Alicia's room, his eyes filled with tears. Quickly he went to her bedside and kissed her gently on the forehead. His son lay sleeping peacefully in her arms. Olan was overjoyed.

"You did us well, my darling," he whispered to Alicia. "We have a beautiful baby. I love you both so much."

"Shall we stick with our first name choice?" Alicia asked.

"Yes. Let's stick with the name Albert," Olan replied.

Olan stayed a few more hours in the hospital room with Alicia. They chatted about next steps and their future with a new baby while Albert slept peacefully. Soon Olan left the hospital and cruised along the dimly lit streets of Trombago. It was a humid night. It had rained earlier in the day, and a light fog lingered over the island now that night had fallen.

It wasn't surprising that the roads were free of traffic. The islanders typically stayed off the roads whenever there was fog. Olan hummed a merry tune as he drove home. He was grateful to God for his newborn son and for his wife. He was so thankful that the delivery had gone well, and that his seven-pound baby boy was healthy.

A month later Myrna gave birth to an eight-pound baby boy. She had labored for almost twelve hours and Greff had been fretful during the entire labor period. After pacing back and forth at the hospital for five hours, he had called Olan.

"Hey Olan," Greff began. "I'm at the hospital with Myrna. Man, it's been ten hours and she is still in labor."

"Hey man. Don't worry. That hospital is the best and the doctor she has is a good one," Olan replied. "Tell you what, I'll come by and wait with you. I'll be there in an hour."

"Alright my brother," Greff replied with a sigh. "See you soon."

When Olan arrived at the hospital he found Greff sitting in the waiting room with his head bowed and his fingers locked behind his neck. Olans' heart began to pound. Fearing the worst he took a deep breath, waited for his heartbeat to slow down, and then walked over to Greff.

"Greff," he said softly.

Greff looked up. He looked tired and strained.

"Hey my brother," Greff replied.

"How's it going?' Olan asked.

Greff sighed.

"It's still a waiting game. She seems to be in a lot of pain," he said.

At that moment a nurse approached them.

"Your wife is calling for you," she said to Greff.

Greff immediately stood up, and Olan placed his arm across his shoulders.

"Hey my man. Take a deep breath," Olan said. "It's going to be okay. I'll be right here for you. Just go in there and show strength and confidence. That's what Myrna needs right now."

Olan grabbed a magazine and settled down in a comfortable chair across from the television. The evening news was in progress and a segment on the latest political developments caught his attention. The government of Trombago had established a new agency to oversee the construction activities on the island. The agency had full authority to approve or decline applications for the construction of buildings based on a stringent set of criteria including the submission of approved plans and disclosures specific to the suppliers of building materials and the human resources to be used on the projects. Olan had no doubt that the establishment of this agency had been a long time in the making. Furthermore he was sure that while some people would welcome government involvement in construction activities, others would definitely be against it.

Olan rose, walked over to the vending machine, and selected a can of orange soda. He hoped all was well with Greff and Myrna. Sitting down once again, he thumbed through the magazine he had selected and yawned. As he did so, he began to feel drowsy. There wasn't much in the magazine to hold his interest, but at least there were other magazines available to him.

"Hey Olan; Olan."

Olan felt someone shaking him. Realizing that he had been sleeping, he opened his eyes and looked up into Greffs' beaming face.

"Olan, it's a boy! I have a big bouncing eight-pound baby boy!" Greff shouted.

Olan leapt up from his chair and, grabbing Greffs' palm with one hand and the back of his neck with the other, he pulled Greff to him.

"Congratulations my man!"

Greff sighed and sat down.

"How is Myrna?" Olan asked.

"She is fine, but very tired. In fact, she nodded off to sleep before I left the room. The baby is sleeping too," Greff replied.

"What will you name him?" Olan asked.

"We don't know as yet. We asked Myrnas' father to give us a name," Greff replied.

Two weeks later Myrnas' father took his grandson in his arms and named him Grant.

15

The years went by and the two families grew closer to each other. Albert and Grant had become inseparable. They had developed a rare brotherly relationship. Albert was at the top of the class and got an A in every subject. He had a very honest and mannerly personality, which somehow made him vulnerable to bullying. Grant, on the other hand, was bold and assertive and had developed a keen interest in sports. He was by no means a slouch in his studies – his mother made sure of that – but he was a real sports enthusiast. He constantly did push-ups and squats and ran laps. Grant was very protective of Albert. He always came to Alberts' defense whenever other kids tried to bully him.

One day at school Albert was sitting on a bench during lunch break when a group of five boys walked over to him.

"Hey twit," one of the boys said.

Albert did not look at them.

The group of boys hurled insults and degrading remarks at Albert. One of them hit him on the head, and another kicked him on the shin. Albert stood up and tried to fight back, but he was outnumbered.

Some younger children in the schoolyard saw what was happening and ran to get a teacher. These children met Grant coming out of the school building and told him what was happening. Grant sped to the scene and immediately began to defend Albert.

Albert became more courageous now that Grant was with him. He and Grant fought the boys with such intensity that in no time the odds were even. It was then that some teachers arrived and put an end to the fighting. All the fighting boys were led to the principals' office and given detention.

Soon it was summer, and Albert registered for boxing and weight-lifting classes. He also worked, alongside Grant, at the Trifecta estate. These activities kept Albert busy all summer and helped him to develop his physical strength and prowess.

One evening the boys sat under a tree exchanging ideas about what school would be like when it reopened the following week. Albert speculated that the boys who had bullied him might be planning to bully him again.

"Nah. I don't think so," Grant said. "That's over. The principal knows now."

The first day back at school was a rainy one. It had started to rain late Sunday evening and had continued throughout the night. Despite the rain, Albert and Grant were excited about returning to school. They had two years remaining until graduation and knew that these last two years were critical.

The rain slowed down soon after they arrived at school on Monday and stopped completely by the time they had their mid-morning break. Overall their first day back at school was an enjoyable one even though they were given a lot of homework. They dedicated themselves to completing all assignments that night and felt satisfied that they had gotten off to a good start.

Because Albert and Grant got off to a good start, their school year was a productive one. They both excelled in all subjects and built new friendships. To their surprise, they had gained new respect from all the children at the school. They had even become friends with the five boys who had fought with them the prior year. These boys showed a new deference to Albert, and Albert was kind enough to help some of them with some of their subjects. Alberts' teacher was pleased with the leadership qualities he demonstrated and encouraged him in that direction.

As the final school year approached, Alberts' and

Grants' parents decided to start planning their boys' future. One Friday night, while enjoying dinner at the Himda Resort, their discussion centered on the careers that their boys would pursue. Olan and Alicia wanted Albert to become a lawyer, but they had wisely left him to choose a career without their influence.

"For four months we were becoming more and more anxious," Olan explained. "Albert had not made a choice one way or the other. Then suddenly last Thursday he rushed in from school bursting with a combination of exhilaration and indignation."

"We had never seen him that way before," Alicia interjected. "I asked him what had happened."

"That was when he told us that he and Grant had just witnessed an incident of police brutality that had left him quite distressed," Olan continued. "He explained that two policemen had badly beaten a man into helplessness, and that a group of civilians had to intervene. According to one of the onlookers, the man had been involved with one of the policemens' girlfriend. Supposedly, even though this policeman was married, he and his fellow officer wanted to teach the man a lesson."

"At that point in the story Alberts' expression had changed from one of indignation to one of exhilaration. He then explained that he decided that he wanted to become a lawyer because he realized that injustice needed to be fought," Alicia chimed in.

"I remember Grant mentioning that incident to us last week," Myrna said. "Wow. It is amazing how that incident helped Albert to decide."

"Grant has made up his mind to become a doctor. His philosophy has always been that medicine and physical care should be a priority in human existence," Greff said.

The parents soon realized that choosing a profession was easy compared to choosing a country to pursue the education needed for the profession. Germany would be an ideal country for Grant to pursue doctoral studies since

Germany was advanced in medical research and sciences. The United States of America would be ideal for Albert to pursue legal studies. Both young men, however, did not welcome the thought of being oceans apart. Separation weighed heavily on their minds, but they submitted applications for admission to colleges in the respective countries.

Being preoccupied with application deadlines and thoughts of separation, the young men and their parents had overlooked the need to evaluate options for financing their studies and living arrangements. After they submitted applications they realized the financial challenges involved and decided that alternatives had to be considered. Myrna contacted an aunt who resided in the United States and explained the situation to her.

"I would be happy to do all I can to assist both young men," Aunt Enid said.

Aunt Enid was a retired school principal and lived with her two grandchildren since her husbands' death. She welcomed the opportunity to not only help, but to strengthen family ties.

As a result, Grant submitted applications to medical schools in the United States, and everyone looked forward to hearing from the colleges.

16

lbert and Grant were accepted into top colleges in the United States. They had been granted scholarships, and their parents were proud. They were treated to an elaborate farewell party at which almost everyone gave a verbal toast, some gave speeches, and still others extended one-on-one congratulations to the young men. The celebration included dancing and continued into the wee hours of the next morning. Later that day Albert and Grant bade farewell to their parents amidst hugs and admonitions to be on their best behavior and to write often.

When Albert and Grant arrived in the United States, they received a warm welcome from Aunt Enid. It wasn't long before she realized that the young men were focused, mannerly and talented. She wrote letters to their parents, expressing just how pleased she was with them. Among other things, she wrote that in her many years of teaching she had never been associated with anyone quite as exemplary as Albert and Grant.

The years passed and, taking Aunt Enids' advice, the young men applied for and obtained United States citizenship even though Grant was at first reluctant since he wanted to do research in remote areas of the world. But Grant quickly overcame his reluctance when he realized that he had to apply for another scholarship in order to complete his medical studies in the United States.

The young men worked hard and planned to celebrate their graduation with a visit to Trombago. They obtained part-time employment and saved much of their earnings so that they could also treat Aunt Enid to a vacation there.

Finally graduation day came. Grants' and Alberts' parents were not present at the ceremony, but Aunt Enid proudly represented them and enthusiastically shared details and pictures of the event with them.

Alberts' parents met Grant and Albert at the airport when they arrived in Trombago with Aunt Enid to celebrate their graduation and enjoy their well-deserved vacation. On the drive home both Albert and Grant were amazed at how much the island had developed. There were many new homes, two-story buildings and shopping centers. Many of the previously paved roads had been repaved with resilient petroleum asphalt, and many of the original dirt roads were now paved with the same asphalt.

Aunt Enid was awestruck. She had been accustomed to seeing tall New York City buildings juxtaposed in maze-like arrangements, and one and two-story homes that were constructed with barely twenty feet between them. On the island, however, most of the buildings and homes were one story, with only the professional buildings, hotels and resorts rising to two stories. Aunt Enid was also intrigued by the beauty of the Caribbean sea and the vast expanses of land with assorted agriculture, wild-life, or farms with a variety of farm animals.

Soon Albert and Grant were brought up to date with the developments in their families. Olan and Alicia were now the proud owners of a finance company and were instrumental in the growth and development of the island. Many of the improvements on the island, including the modernized roads, could be traced directly or indirectly to their finance company.

Myrnas' father had passed away the year before and had left her a legacy of his fleet of buses. In addition, Greff and Myrna had been fortunate to purchase the resort that they loved so much. The Himda Resort had been destroyed in an unfortunate fire the year before, and the owner had been so distraught that he decided to sell the premises instead of restoring it and running it once more with the memory of loved ones who had died in the fire. Greff and Myrna had bought what remained of the resort and restored it to full operation. Most of its' original design, including the fitness center, night club and ballroom facilities, were retained and the picturesque and breathtaking view of the ocean, mountains and hills remained as a focal point.

Albert and Grant were honored at a party in celebration of their educational accomplishments. Family and friends gathered at the Himda Resort and happily shared in the warmth, love and camaraderie that the occasion fostered. Albert and Grant were touched by the sincere love and congratulations they received and were heartened by the fact that their parents were proud of them.

As the days went by Albert and Grant decided to visit their old high school. They were amazed to find out that two of the boys with whom they had fought were now teachers at the school. In addition, the prior vice principal was now the principal. He provided them with a tour of the classes that were in session. They were impressed by the progress that the school had made.

It was good to spend time with family and friends, and Albert, Grant and Aunt Enid enjoyed their vacation immensely. They were able to relax, socialize, and strengthen important bonds that they would keep for a lifetime. Nonetheless Albert and Grant looked forward to returning to the United Stated to forge ahead with their careers.

17

Years passed during which both Albert and Grant succeeded in many areas of their lives. Grant completed his internship and started his private medical practice. He married Amy Leache – a slender, dark-haired American, with a beautiful face. Amy was also a medical practitioner.

Grant was a devoted husband; always helpful and attentive. He was still active in sports and always maintained his physique. He and Amy were blessed with a boy and a girl whom they named Wren and Mary, respectively. They watched their children grow, never failing to be firm when necessary.

It did not come as a surprise when both Wren and Mary expressed their desire to become doctors. Their parents had encouraged them, of course, but they had not forced or coerced them.

Wren and Mary pursued their doctoral studies with passion. The fact that their parents were doctors inspired them, and enabled them to gain supplemental knowledge outside of college lectures and labs. This buttressed their understanding and success in a remarkable way. Wren chose to do his internship in the United States while Mary decided to relocate to South America to pursue medical research. This was because South America was not only tranquil, but also had an abundance of herbs suitable for medical research.

It proved to be difficult for Mary to settle in South America. Many of the conveniences she had been accustomed to in the United States were not available there. In addition the natives were skeptical of her, and of foreigners altogether. But Mary was tough and resolute. Quitting was not an option for her. She gradually learned the values and customs of the South American people and began to find her comfort zone. Her big turning point came when natives were cutting down trees and clearing an area for farming. While they were doing this some trees fell into the river. Soon fish began to die, some young children died, and most people suffered from bouts of vomiting. Mary decided to do some research. She tested samples of all the trees, vines and shrubs in the area. She determined that the Vitmo vine had a poisonous component to it. She further determined that this vine was attached to the trees that had fallen into the river.

With the help of the South American government Mary instructed everyone to clear the Vitmo vines from the river, and to keep it away from streams and farmland. In addition all persons were forbidden to use water from the river until the government granted clearance to do so.

Mary proceeded to do extensive research on the Vitmo vine. She determined that the vine was poisonous if overused or liquified to a high degree of potency. However if it was used in limited dosages, and at low degrees of potency, it could be a powerful antidote. Mary identified and extracted its antidotal component and obtained government authorization to develop and market the antidote in South America.

Mary had not only fostered health and wellness; she had helped to make the community a safer place. Although she was still regarded by some South Americans as being a foreigner, she became accepted by many as a person of goodwill.

Albert married Jean Hill, a very pretty blonde American, with a secure profession as financial advisor at the Stock Exchange. They had one daughter, Adrean, who had blossomed over the years and was now a B+ student in high school.

Albert gained employment with the Equal Rights

Agency established to oversee the welfare, progress, rights and protection of American citizens. This was an ideal position for him, given his educational background and the pledge he had made to himself on the day when he had observed policemen beating a man in Trombago.

Peter Follek, the head of the Agency, was a tall elderly man with a non-smiling countenance and he possessed only a high school diploma. He had been a police inspector before being employed at the Agency. Peter had always been involved in shady deals and had been placed into his current position as a result of always calling in favors owed to him. He was fortunate to be assigned efficient, reliable, and productive Agency staff who performed their duties with the utmost dedication. Despite their commitment, however, most of his staff did not like him because they realized that he still carried out shady deals and could not be trusted. Ironically, because Peter had such reliable staff, he had spare time to make a lot of private deals for kickbacks and favors.

One of Peters' staff members – Evin Flek, the financial controller – was regarded as Peters' favorite. He was very good with numbers and was a genius at balancing Agency finances and preparing audit reports. Peter always showed Evin a lot of favor, and some staff members regarded Evin as the Boss' spy.

On his first day at work, Albert arrived early. Peter took him around to the various departments and introduced him as the newest member of the Agency. Then he took him to a small, modest office.

"This is where you will perform your duties. The office to your left is Noras' office. She has been employed with the Agency for many years and is assigned to give you all the information and assistance you'll need," said Peter. "Come, I'll introduce you to her."

"Nora this is Albert. He is our new man here and will be working closely with you. Give him all the help he needs," Peter said.

"Thank you sir," said Albert.

Peter left the office without closing the door, and after closing it himself, Albert approached Nora. She got up as he approached her.

"Please be seated," Albert said to her.

Nora was a middle-aged woman with a subtle charm and an air of competence and reliability. She reminded Albert of Grants' mother Myrna.

"I'm going to rely on you a lot," he said, "and I hope I won't be too imposing."

"You won't be at all," Nora replied. "I'll assist in any way I can."

"First I'll need my full job description," Albert said.

"Here it is sir," Nora replied, handing him a folder.

"Thanks. Call me Albert," said Albert, taking the folder. "I'm going to head over to my office now."

"Ok," Nora replied, "let me know if you need anything else."

At the door Albert paused and looked back at her.

"Is everyone here as nice as you are?" he asked.

"I guess," she replied, "but I'm sure that you'll find out for yourself."

Once in his office Albert began assessing his duties – Riot Acts, Peaceful Demonstrations, Civil Liberties and Abuses…. I'll have to go to the library to research regulations related to some of these; it's like going back to school, he thought.

When Albert arrived home, Jean and Adrean greeted him at the door. They had been anxiously waiting to hear about his first day on the job.

"So how did everything go today?" Jean asked while they were having dinner.

"Good, I guess. It's sort of what I really want to do, but a lot of legal framework is involved. Guess I'll have to do a lot of research and study the legal aspects of it all," Albert replied. "The Chief Administrator with whom I will be working seems to be a very nice person, very efficient and

45

reliable. I like her."

"Hmmm, you like her," Jean remarked with a laugh. "One day on the job and you are already flirting."

Albert laughed.

"You will like her too. She reminds me so much of Grants' mother, although she is younger. She seems to have Myrnas' personality," he said.

"That's interesting," said Jean.

"This lamb is so delicious honey," said Albert. He smiled. "I'll do the dishes tonight."

"Oh no honey, it's ok," Jean replied. "You just relax."

"Can I do them?" Adrean asked.

"Ok, but you are not going to get paid," Albert replied.

Adrean laughed and pinched his nose. Now seventeen, she was showing a great deal of maturity and responsibility.

18

Over the years Albert became very proficient in his job. With Noras' assistance, he tackled some of the most arduous assignments in the Agency and exceeded Agency goals. Nora developed a deep respect for his devotion, his honesty, and his strong concern for the welfare of others. She had never before detected these qualities in anyone in the Agency.

Soon Albert was assigned to a case where a developer wanted to build a shopping mall in an area designated for residential use. The majority of the residents in this area were middle-class, and a few of them were low-income residents.

Albert conducted extensive investigation and determined that the residents had been subjected to threats, coercion, deception, bribes and blackmail, which resulted in some of them selling their properties to the developer. Most of the residents, however, had stood their ground. They loved their homes and neighborhood and refused to sell below market value, or at any price for that matter. Suddenly, over a period of two weeks, many of the homes were set on fire. Fortunately none of the residents were seriously injured, although they suffered property damages.

The residents set vigils throughout the community. Finally they caught three men in the act of setting another fire. They retaliated and, in the ensuing riot, the three men were beaten so badly that when the police arrived they arrested some of the residents and charged them with assault. The men were admitted to the hospital, and two of them were listed in critical condition.

When the riot incident was reported to the Agency for investigation Alberts' first instinct was to make sure that the three arsonists were under tight security. He became suspicious when law enforcement insisted that the matter was in their jurisdiction and wanted to take custody of the three men. Albert retorted that the civil rights and liberties of the three men were his responsibility, and that the men would remain in his custody until they recovered. He realized that he needed information from each of them before handing them over to anyone.

Albert assembled his team for the investigation. Nora was assigned to liaise with all internal departments and external governmental agencies to facilitate the teams' work. Based on her recommendation, two of the most trusted and reliable men in the Agency were assigned to the case. Blair Warner was assigned to investigate the residents' complaints, and Jake Timmer was given the task of investigating the three arsonists as well as determining who had enlisted them to commit the crime.

Albert provided Nora, Blair and Jake with clear instructions.

"Document and classify your observations and communications in detail. I will research property ownerships, titles, deeds, interested purchasers, and recent purchases pertaining to that neighborhood. Nora will send us a biweekly meeting reminder. At our meetings we will review all findings and update the status of the case," he said.

19

Grant and Amy were carrying out a prosperous medical practice. They had acquired a spacious office with four private rooms for examinations and a separate room for their lab work. Two receptionists and three nurses complemented them as they provided medical services to the community.

Office hours were from nine o'clock to seven o'clock, Monday through Friday. Amy and Grant staggered their hours so that Amy started working at nine o'clock and Grant arrived at eleven o'clock. This arrangement allowed them to see all their patients each day, as well as spend quality time with each other. Grant and Amy looked forward to their time together and their social activities with Albert and Jean, but these times were short-lived. Misfortune befell them in a peculiar way.

One evening one of Amys' receptionists was having trouble with her car and Amy offered to drive her home. As usual, she kissed Grant on her way out.

"What's for supper?" he asked.

"Leftovers and water," Amy replied.

After saying goodnight to the staff, Amy and her receptionist walked to Amys' car.

"What's wrong with your car?" Amy asked, as she entered the main street from the parking lot.

"The battery, I guess," replied the receptionist, "but my husband will take care of it. He is very good with his hands and I can depend on him."

"We are very fortunate women to have such reliable men by our sides," Amy replied.

Those were, unfortunately, the last words Amy spoke. It was at that point that an oncoming vehicle driven by an elderly woman swerved to avoid hitting a turtle, crossed the dividing line in the road, and ran headfirst into Amys' car.

It was a five-car collision. Amy's car was pinned on each side between two cars and also hit from the back. Amy and her receptionist died instantly.

While it was relatively easy for the cars on each side of Amys' car to be removed, it was four hours before rescue workers were able to retrieve Amys' body and the body of her receptionist from Amys' car. Firstly, they had to remove both the driver and the car that had struck the car behind Amys'. Then they had to remove the driver and passenger from the car directly behind Amys' car. The entire front of that car, including the windshield, had rammed into Amys' car. After removing that car, they were able to remove Amy and her receptionists' crumpled remains.

A total of three people died in the accident, including a seven-year-old boy who had been travelling with the elderly woman. Four persons were severely hurt, and indications were that two of them would be paralyzed for life.

It was way past eight o'clock and Grant had been home for some time. He was becoming concerned that Amy was not yet home. He placed the leftovers on the stove to warm, set the table, and began to make a salad. Soon he heard the front door opening.

"Hi hon! Had a hard time finding the way?" he shouted.

"Sorry dad, it's me," Wren answered.

"Mom's not yet home. She drove home one of our receptionists who had a car problem," Grant responded. "How was your day?"

"So busy. I'm bushed," Wren replied.

Wren flopped, landed on the sofa, and turned on the TV.

"Look at this crash!" he exclaimed. "No one can live through this!"

Grant poured two glasses of wine and was preparing to sit down and watch the news with Wren when the doorbell rang.

"There's mom now. Guess she stopped for groceries?"

Wren surmised.

When Grant opened the door, he saw two policemen.

"May we come in?" one of them asked.

"Sure," Grant replied.

"We have some very sad news," said the other policeman.

The accident was still being aired on the TV. Grant looked at the TV, and then at the policemen.

"The accident?" Grant asked in a whisper-like tone. He felt short of breath.

The policeman nodded.

"Yes," he replied.

"How bad?" Grant asked fearfully.

"They didn't survive. I'm sorry. Their deaths were instantaneous," the policeman replied.

Grant felt his body sway and braced himself by pressing his palm against the wall.

"I am so sorry. They died on impact," the policeman said solemnly.

Grant hung his head and his body quivered. It was as though a cold wind had entered into it. He heard Wren gasp and he walked over to him. Wren got up from the couch and hugged his father.

"If it is not too much for you right now, we would like you to come with us to identify the bodies. We can take you there and back," the policeman continued.

In a short while Grant and Wren arrived at the police precinct. As they had anticipated, it was not difficult for them to identify both bodies. Although the women were bruised and battered, their features were identifiable.

Grants' inner strength was put to the test. He notified his mother, father, Mary, and Amys' family members, and began making funeral arrangements.

News of Amys' death was reported in local newspapers and aired on television and radio stations. Funeral services were also broadcasted on all media. As a result, the funeral was well-attended. It reminded Albert of a statesmans' funeral. Mary arrived from South America to share in the love and unity afforded by family and friends. She mourned deeply since she had been away from home for many months and had missed spending time with her mother, but Grant and Wren assuaged her emotions with an outpouring of love, advice and consolation.

Albert performed the eulogy. His many references to Amys' character and achievements will long be remembered. He shared the fact that many people referred to Amy as "my doctor" – a testimony that Amy was not just a doctor, she was the peoples' doctor.

"Yes, Amy has passed away. She might be dead, but to most of us she will never die because she will always remain in our hearts and minds," Albert concluded.

Sad times can affect ones' morale and Albert was determined to make sure that it would not affect Grants'. In the ensuing months he and Jean visited Grant twice, sometimes three times, each week. Sometimes he would take Grant out to dinner, and on many occasions he spent several hours at home with him and Wren.

20

Early one afternoon the hospital called Albert to let him know that one of the arsonists was responsive and might be able to talk. It turned out that the driver, Ted, had awakened. He explained to Albert that his job was only to drive the vehicle to the location.

"So, who paid to have the fire set?" Albert asked.

"I know someone did because Butt told me that he was paid seven thousand for the job," Ted replied.

"And who is Butt?" Albert asked.

"Butt is the guy who paid me to drive," Ted replied.

"And who is the third guy?" Albert asked.

"He is the torcher," Ted replied. "I only know him as Torch. Butt uses different men, but he likes Torch the most. Torch might know who paid to have the fire set."

Once he was back at the office Albert met with his team and discussed the information that he, Jake, Blair and Nora had gathered so far.

"We still need more information in order to get to the bottom of this," Albert concluded. "Butt is probably not going to freely give us information. He seems to be in charge of the arson team since he pays the men. Torch would be a better target for us when he is well enough to talk. We should also keep pressing the driver – Ted."

At the end of the meeting Nora suggested to Albert that he should start Kung Fu and Karate lessons similar to those that Jake was taking. She did not have to explain why. Alberts' instincts were aroused.

Over the next few weeks Albert and Jake visited the hospital frequently in order to not miss the chance to question Butt and Torch as soon as they were conscious. Eventually the doctor gave them the go-ahead to talk with Butt.

"You guys are cops?" Butt asked, as Albert and Jake entered his room.

"No," Albert replied. "We are from the Equal Rights Agency."

"So, you are lawyers?" asked Butt.

"No, but if you want a lawyer we can get you one," Albert answered.

"I don't need no lawyer. Lawyers are just a bunch of crooks. I don't need one," Butt retorted.

Jake and Albert exchanged glances.

"So, what prompted you to set the fires?" Albert asked.

"Just the thought of it. I'm a Fire Bug, didn't you know?" Butt replied.

"And you almost got yourself killed for doing it. Did someone pay you or ask you to set the fires?" Albert continued.

"I just love the sight of fires. It's in my nature," Butt said with a sly smile.

"Well you were lucky this time. You almost lost your life," said Albert. "Do you want to file a complaint against the people that hurt you?"

"No, not at all. I don't believe in your court systems," Butt replied.

"Maybe the people that got hurt or lost their valuables might file a lawsuit against you," Jake interjected.

"That's too bad. I was told that no one was living there. The homes were supposed to be empty," Butt replied.

"And who told you that?" Albert asked. "I'm sure whoever told you that is going to say that you're lying."

"Jim wouldn't dare say that. I have too much on him," Butt muttered.

"And who is Jim?" Jake asked.

"I'm not saying anything more," Butt snapped. "Please go."

"Okay then, but we will be talking with you again soon," said Albert.

"So, you are sure that you do not want a lawyer?" Jake

asked.

"I am as sure as I am sure that I am lying here. Lawyers are for fools," Butt replied.

The next day Albert and Jake met with Blair and Nora to compare notes and discuss the status of the investigation.

"I take it you gentlemen had a busy day in your quest for answers yesterday," said Blair.

"We sure did," said Jake.

"Did you get all our conversations on tape?" Albert asked Jake.

"Yep," said Jake, pressing the play button.

"This Butt person is really trying to be a tough guy, but somehow he isn't very smart. We got some useful information out of him, without him even realizing it," said Albert. "We now have to focus on finding out who Jim is. Jim has to be an important person in this scheme. I believe he is a go-between."

"Remember, Butt said that he has a lot on Jim," Jake interjected. "They have to be close, maybe even partners."

"Maybe the residents can shed some light on who Jim is," said Blair. "I will look closely into that possibility."

Jake and Blair bumped into Norm as they left the meeting room.

"Hi Norm," Jake said in a loud voice.

"Gentlemen," Norm replied. "Is Albert in there?"

"Sure. Go on in. We just finished our meeting," Blair responded.

"Good afternoon sir," Norm said to Albert on entering the room. "This letter came for you. It's personal."

"Thank you," Albert responded, taking the letter. "But please, call me Albert."

"I don't believe you met Norm," Nora said to Albert. "This is Norman Roye. He is a valuable part of our organization."

"Glad to meet you Norm," Albert said. "You can be relaxed around me at all times."

"Thank you sir, and ma'am," Norm replied, and left the room.

"I've seen him around the office a few times before, but never quite figured out his position here," Albert commented.

"He is, like everyone here, quite valuable," Nora responded. "He was a Sargent in the army before being hurt in the war. He is now our Records and Documents Specialist."

"I noticed his slowness in responding when I spoke to him," Albert replied.

"Yes. He suffered a mild shock, stroke, and back injuries. His hearing is a bit impaired. He can hear, but usually hears much better when we raise our voices," said Nora. "Do not be fooled by his minor handicap, however. He is very smart and knows his job. Although somewhat reserved and private, he is intelligent and respectful. Anyway, I am going to head home now. It's getting late."

"Oh," Albert remarked, looking at the letter in his hand. "I almost forgot. Wait a minute please. Your input might be needed here."

Albert was right about needing input from Nora. The letter was from the Chief of Detectives. It read, in part:

Sorry to hear about your unpleasant encounters. I'm sure we share the same commitment… Information shared between us could be very helpful to the case of the Denham City residents… Let's meet in a social environment and try to create a better relationship…

"What the hell does he mean?" Albert said with a frown. "Create a better relationship? I don't know if I can trust this man. It seems as though he might want to probe my mind. Maybe he has a hidden agenda."

"Take it easy," Nora replied. "Meet with him. Maybe he is genuine. You never know, he might have something you can use. In meeting with him just keep your wits about you, talk less than he does and, if necessary, don't talk about the case. In addition, try not to eat too much and make milk your beverage of choice instead of alcohol. Be assertive and forthright. He will admire and respect you for that. Have a nice weekend. Got to go."

"Ok Nora, have a nice weekend. Thanks a lot," Albert replied.

After Nora left Albert read the letter over and over, wondering what the Chief of Detectives had in mind. Finally, with a sigh, he decided to go home.

While waiting for the elevator Albert saw Norm coming his way.

"Hello again," said Norm with a smile.

The elevator door opened, and they got in.

"Thanks again for the letter," Albert said in a loud voice.

"I'm glad that I could help," Norm replied. "It was really nothing."

"It means a lot to me. Not everyone is so polite and efficient these days," said Albert.

The elevator door opened, and the men got off.

"Thanks again, and have a nice weekend," said Albert, extending his hand.

The men shook hands.

"Same to you," Norm replied, thinking that Albert seemed to be alright but that he would wait awhile to see if he was genuine or was just being polite. It seemed to Norm that Albert gave respect to everyone and, in so doing, got respect in return.

21

The following Friday Blair left the office thinking about visiting Denham City over the weekend to try and get more information about the fires. He went to bed that night mulling over the possibility that he could dig up some key information.

By Saturday afternoon his mind was made up. At four o'clock he set out for Denham City. As he entered the main areas that had been devasted by the fires, he noticed that some of the homes had been restored and that others were being worked on. He passed many residents who were outside taking care of the neighborhood. Then he began driving through the commercial area of the town and passed a couple of upper class restaurants before stopping at a middle-income diner.

The inside of the diner was relatively nice, with several tables and chairs arranged for dining as well as a cocktail bar for those choosing not to dine. Blair sat down at the bar.

"How may I help you?" the bartender asked. He didn't seem very friendly.

"May I have a beer?" Blair replied.

"Any special brand?" the bartender asked.

"Miller, please," Blair replied.

Just as Blair began to sip his beer, two men appeared beside him. Blair was sure that the bartender had sent them over to him.

"Are you one of those guys trying to buy us out?" one of the men asked. He seemed demanding, but not very threatening.

"If so we are not selling, and we do not want you guys around here," the other man interjected.

Before Blair had a chance to answer, the owner of the diner walked in with his wife and a couple.

"What's going on Bing?" the owner said to the bartender.

Bing whispered something to the owner, who then walked over to Blair.

"Is it true that you are trying to buy these people out?" the owner asked Blair.

The owner then took a closer look at Blair.

"My God, you are the man from the Agency! I have seen you on the news. Jake or Blake, right?" the owner exclaimed.

"Yes I am from the Agency. I am Blair," Blair responded.

"Yes, yes. Blair. That's it. My apologies. I am Mike, the owner of the diner. So what brings you here?"

The two men standing beside Blair looked at each other with puzzled expressions. Blair glanced questioningly at them.

"My guys are not violent," Mike assured him, "but they are concerned and protective. What can we do to help you out? Come, join us at our table."

The table was positioned so that Mike could always see all the patrons in the diner. He introduced his wife and friends to Blair and then fetched a chair for him.

"Here, pick something from the menu," he said, handing Blair a menu. "Our choices are always the same."

"I'll have whatever you are having," Blair replied. "I'm pretty sure that I'll enjoy it."

"So, tell me, what brings you here today?" Mike asked.

"My Agency has run into a snag. The men who set the fires are not talking, but somehow the name Jim came up. We have no clue who the hell Jim is. We are hoping that somebody here might know," Blair replied.

"So many Jims around, it's hard to really associate any of them with those guys, but I can ask around. Somebody should have an idea," Mike said.

"Wait a minute," Mikes' friend interjected, "Raymond should know. He is always talking about this guy that works with the developer who is interested in buying property around here. I think he said his name is Jimray. I can telephone Raymond, and you can talk with him."

"Just a minute. Let me find out if Bing knows anything," Mike replied. "Hey Bing!" He beckoned Bing over to the table. "Do you know of a guy called Jim?"

"No," Bing replied.

"Or Jimray?" Mike queried.

"The name Jimray rings a bell…." Bing concentrated a moment. "Oh yes, there was this guy here from some development company. He was looking to buy properties. I think his name is Jimray. I almost threw his ass out of here. He left a business card. I will see if I can find it."

Bing went back to the bar.

"Bing will find it," Mike remarked. "He never throws anything away."

Soon Bing returned with the business card.

"Here it is. I hope this helps," he said.

Blair took the business card. It read:

Jimray Burns. Acquisition Manager. Loop Development.

"This is more than just help," Blair said, nodding. "We have just uncovered who Jim really is. I cannot thank you all enough."

Mike signaled to the two men who had been antagonistic to Blair earlier. The men joined them and were introduced to Blair.

"Blair is working on our behalf. Please look out for him," Mike said to them.

"Let me get your business card Blair," Bing said. "I will call you if anything comes up to help this matter. It's our welfare and we will do everything to help to protect it."

"You can rest assured that my Agency will be doing everything to uphold and protect the rights of the citizens here," said Blair.

The group shared another bottle of wine. Then Blair realized that it was getting late and he had a far way to go.

"We wish you could stay a little while longer," Mike said.

"But visit us again soon and bring your friends – Jake and the other guy."

"Albert," Blair reminded him.

"Yes, Albert. How could I forget?" Mike chuckled.

"Once again, thanks for everything, and especially for dinner. It was absolutely delicious," Blair said.

Monday is going to be a very interesting day at work, Blair said to himself as he drove home. I can't wait to see the look of amazement on Alberts' face when he hears that we finally know who Jim is.

Blair rested well that night. His sleep was completely uninterrupted. Then he spent Sunday relaxing and anticipating the next steps in the investigation. Monday seemed to be taking a very long time to arrive.

22

Blair was the first one from the team to arrive at the Agency on Monday. He reorganized his desk, placed documents in file folders, labeled the folders and filed the folders in alphabetical order in his desk drawer, but he kept his eye on the clock the whole time.

It seemed to be a very long time before Nora arrived.

"Good morning!" Blair exclaimed.

"Good morning Blair. I've never seen you here this early. Had a restless night?" Nora replied.

"On the contrary. I slept like a baby. We have to have a meeting this morning. It is very important," Blair replied.

"It will have to wait an hour or so. Albert is in an early morning meeting with the Boss," Nora responded.

At that moment Jake walked in.

"Good morning," he said. "How did you guys spend your weekend?"

"Good morning. I had a great weekend," said Blair.

"So did I," Nora said.

"You seem rather happy for a Monday morning," Jake said to Blair.

"I have some very important news and I can hardly wait to break it to the team. We are waiting for Albert to meet with us," Blair responded.

"Where is he by the way?" Jake asked.

"Albert's in a meeting with the Boss," Nora replied.

"What the hell did he do wrong?" Jake asked, with a chuckle.

Jake headed for his office, made a few phone calls, scribbled some notes in the palm of his hand and then sat back to enjoy his coffee. Soon he was summoned to meet with the team.

"Let's get to it gentlemen," Nora said. "Blair is going to

have a heart attack if we wait any longer."

Jake chuckled.

"Here is an aspirin," he said, and pretended to retrieve one from his pocket.

"You're the one that might need it after I give you the good news," Blair replied.

"Out with it man, the suspense is killing me," Jake blurted.

"Well, I found our mystery man Jim," Blair said proudly.

"You what? Where is he? I don't see anyone but us here," Jake replied.

"Here, now you do," Blair retorted, handing Jake the business card he had received from Bing. "Over the weekend I did some dining in the neighborhood where the fires took place. The owner of Easy Diner invited me over to his table for dinner. The bartender, who is adept at remembering people and retaining information, was a big help. He remembered someone who he felt could possibly be Jim. He had retained that card which he got from the person he thinks could be Jim."

"Darn it man. Do you ever sleep?" Jake asked.

Nora took a very long look at the business card.

"Loop Development again," she muttered. "This is not the first time that they have been implicated in something like this."

"Ok, let's be tight-lipped about Loop Development and Jim as we scrutinize them secretly," Albert said. "Good work Blair."

"Yes. Good work Blair. You deserve a raise, but it won't come from me," Jake said with a look at Albert.

Jake opened his hand and read from his palm.

"The driver," he read, "is to be released into the custody of law enforcement, and we have no control over that matter. It was ordered by the Chief of Police who cited that he committed a criminal offense and should be arrested."

Wetting a paper towel with water from his water bottle, Jake used it to wipe his palm clean. Albert and Blair started laughing.

"Do not laugh," Nora said. "By writing in his hand, and wiping it clean after sharing information, Jake has just shown us something which we all should be using from now on."

Albert had been noticeably reserved throughout the meeting.

"When I met with the Boss this morning he requested that we keep him briefed on the case we are working on. He wants a bi-weekly briefing," he revealed.

Nora took a sharpie and wrote the rest of Alberts' statement in the palm of her hand. He is not going to get all our findings; he can always get our edited findings, she wrote. Then she took a paper towel, wet it, and wiped her palm clean.

"You guys are very good," Albert said. "Nothing to trace back to. Anyway, I'll keep him briefed, as he wants me to. Anything to make the Boss happy."

"Well that is it for our meeting today. Let's continue our work and see if we can come up with more links and conclusions," Albert concluded.

After Blair and Jake left the room Albert turned to Nora.

"Something is going on that I just cannot put my finger on," he said.

"Maybe I can help," Nora said.

"The letter from the Chief of Detectives; the driver being released into the custody of law enforcement; the Boss wants to be briefed; there is a connection," Albert replied.

"The Boss was Assistant to the Chief of Police before he came to work here, and many were suspicious that they both had some deal going on between them. There was an investigation into their activities, but it was hurriedly swept under the rug. It has been said that the Police Chief used his influence to get our Boss his position here," Nora said.

Albert began to pace the floor.

"It is believed, in some circles, that our Boss and the

Police Chief keep incriminating information on each other to use as leverage to get special favors done. In an instance like this, I think someone is calling in a favor," Albert added.

"Keep your wits about you, and your eyes and ears open," Nora replied. "It is possible that the Chief of Police and our Boss are conducting suspicious activities. Clues will surface in some unusual way, and we will eventually have the answers we need."

23

One morning Norm was in the Boss' office, getting documents and notes to be filed and information to be recorded, when Evin Flek walked in.

"Have a seat Evin, we have to talk," Peter said.

Evin looked a bit uneasy.

"Relax Evin. It's nothing to do with you personally. It's Albert I'm worried about," Peter said.

"What is it about him that worries you?" Evin asked, while looking at Norm and wondering about their privacy.

"Oh him. Don't worry about him. He is just a deaf and not too smart nigger. I doubt that he can hear a word we are saying. We would have to be talking really loudly for him to hear a word. But back to Albert, he is a guy that likes to dig deep into things. He is very honest and reliable, but he takes his job too seriously and once he gets hold of something he doesn't let go. I am afraid that one day he is going to dig into our affairs," Peter explained. "So I want you to keep your eyes on him, and your ears tuned in to him, at all times. Do you get what I'm saying?"

"I understand, and you can depend on me," Evin replied.

Evin turned to leave the office.

"Bye Norm," he said.

Norm did not blink an eye, nor did he reply.

"See, I told you he is deaf. Trust me, he did not hear a word," Peter explained. "Oh, where are you going for lunch?"

"I'm meeting up with my wife in a little while," Evin replied.

"Well maybe next time we can grab a bite together. By the way, you can invest more in the Malutica deal, it's getting bigger," Peter said.

"Ok," said Evin, and left the office.

Soon afterwards Peter collected the files he needed for his mid-morning meeting.

"Remember to lock the door when you're through," he said to Norm on the way out of his office. Peter did not get a response from Norm.

A deaf and not too smart nigger is what he thinks of me huh, we'll see about that someday, Norm muttered. Unknown to almost everyone, Norm had been getting therapy for his injuries and his hearing in particular had improved a lot. With the help of his doctor, he had trained very hard. Through the technique of responding to measured tones Norm had practiced pretending not to hear normally pitched sounds when he actually heard them and responding only when the volume or tone was high. So, in essence, his hearing was now very good.

That night Norm kept wondering whether he should tell Albert, or anyone for that matter, what he had overheard. He fell asleep with the decision to keep it to himself for the time being, and just wait instead for the right moment to reveal it.

24

The South American government had erected a lab adjoining the main hospital and Mary was now working there on major medical research, as part of a team of technicians and doctors. Mary had used her influence to help John, one of the boys in the community, gain employment as a janitor and messenger for the hospital. He had lost his parents in the vine incident, had become attached to Mary at first sight, and had found ways to be around her almost all the time. She had encouraged him to always attend school and be diligent in everything he did.

Marys' encouragement had been worthwhile. Johns' diligence was now demonstrated in the way he cleaned up around the lab as well as in the interest he showed in lab work. He would ask questions and sometimes touch the vials. Even though some of the lab technicians became annoyed whenever he touched the vials, they were nonetheless tolerant of him. They understood his curiosity.

As Johns' interest in the lab grew, Mary was inspired. She sent overseas for science books for him to read at nights and helped him to understand those topics that were somewhat advanced for his age. She detected that he would one day be someone of great value in the lab and so she willingly encouraged his involvement there, however minor it might be. She asked that he be allowed to clean the equipment and to sometimes look through the microscope. Soon the entire lab team observed his sustained interest, became aware that he wanted to make medical lab work his profession, and supported his understanding of their work.

After a year, John was trusted with duties that facilitated the teams' medical research. He was delegated work that allowed him to excel. Mary was elated by his accomplishments. Nonetheless she encouraged him to continue his schooling, and to even undertake advanced schooling. The young man pledged that he would do so.

Wren had taken his mothers' position at the doctors' office and had acquired most of her patients, as well as new ones of his own. The office was now a father and son operation and had grown immensely with the addition of new patients and new staff. Wren was also engaged to marry Dale Lurch, the vice principal of the neighborhood high school. He had met Dale when she had brought her mother into the office for a doctors' visit. She was a likeable person who was highly respected in the community.

Dales' parents became closely associated with Grant and was always trying to set him up with dates. Soon Wren began to feel concerned. He began to wonder what would happen to Grant when he got married. He brought up the subject at dinner one Sunday.

"Dad," he said. "Won't you be lonely when Dale and I get married?"

"No Wren, I sure won't. I was somehow hoping that both of you would live here until you can buy yourselves a home. That would be fine with me, and I won't be in your way. As for me being lonely, remember, I am a member of the golf club. In addition, I do have some casual dates. Plus you will still be around, won't you?" Grant replied.

"I will talk with Dale about us living with you for a while. She is just as concerned as I am," Wren replied.

Wren immediately called Dale and discussed Grant's proposal with her. She was in total agreement since, over time, it would put her and Wren on better financial footing. Furthermore, it would diminish their concerns about Grants' welfare.

25

Monday at the Agency was its' typically slow, hard-to-get-moving, kind of day. Albert only had a few phone calls to make and, as usual, some notes to look over. In the afternoon, Norm came in to see him.

"Hi Norm," Albert said, forgetting to raise his voice.

Norm put his hand to his ear.

"How are you?" Albert said with a louder tone.

"Fine thank you sir. This letter just came in for you," Norm replied.

"Thanks a lot, and remember, please call me Albert," Albert said.

The letter was from the Chief of Detectives.

Albert went into Noras' office. She was on the phone and motioned for him to have a seat.

"Ok," Nora spoke into the receiver, "I will bring the wine and cake. See you on Saturday then."

Nora turned her attention to Albert.

"Sorry Albert, what have you got?"

"It's another letter from the Chief of Detectives. He still wants to meet with me," Albert replied.

"By all means go ahead. Did he say where and when the meeting should take place?" Nora asked.

Albert nodded. He handed her the letter.

"Cushions," said Nora. "That is a high-class restaurant. You should be very safe there. But get there before he does and if a table is reserved, select a different one."

Just as Nora had said, Cushions was a top-of-the-line restaurant with a comfortable easy-going atmosphere and lots of privacy for conversations of all kinds. Albert was ushered to a corner table at the back wall of the restaurant when he arrived but requested to be seated at a window table to the left of the entrance instead. He ordered a bottle of wine and made himself comfortable at the table. A short while later he observed the young lady at the check-in desk directing a tall slender man dressed in a suit and tie to his table.

"You must be Albert," the man said when he arrived at Alberts' table. "I am Bill Hall. I sent you those letters. Hope I did not keep you waiting."

"Oh no, not at all," Albert replied. "I got here only a few minutes ago."

Just then their waiter came over with the wine list.

"We're okay," Albert said to him. "We'll share this bottle. We may order another bottle after we finish this one."

"I'll have my usual barbecue chicken meal," Bill instructed the waiter.

"And you sir?" the waiter asked Albert.

"I'll have the baked chicken with white rice and a salad," Albert replied.

Albert took a sip of wine and studied Bill while he poured wine into his glass.

"I notice that you are a bit apprehensive, perhaps uncertain about our first meeting, but let me assure you that I can be trusted," Bill said, without looking up at Albert. "My approach might be a little unorthodox, but I learn a lot from the reaction I get from people. Right now I find you to be an honest, reliable, and fair person."

"You are able to determine all that about me already?" Albert asked.

"I'm a detective, remember?" Bill countered. He took a sip of wine. "Anyway I am going to give you some information that I'm sure will prove to be very useful to you, and I hope that you can work with me on some key issues. Please do not tape anything I am going to tell you or put anything in writing. Keep everything in your brain. It is to your advantage that you do so."

Bill paused, took another sip of wine, and studied Albert with interest. Albert nodded.

"There are some exceptional people working in your Agency – Nora, Blair, Jake, and a few others that I won't name right now. You can fully trust those that I have mentioned and put your confidence in them. The gentleman who gave you my letters – you can put your life in his hands. He is one of a kind. Your boss Peter Follek, however, is a very dangerous and deceitful person. Never take your eyes off him. The same goes for one Evin Flek. Be on your guard around both of them. It so happens that I have to be doing the same with my Police Chief at the precinct. These three men have something going on, and I aim to find out what it is. There is a name that came up that links them together. Have you ever heard of Malutica?"

"No, I've not heard that name before now," Albert replied.

"Well I've heard that name mentioned a few times. It seems to be a connection between my Police Chief and your boss. I have no clue who or what Malutica is but I'm working on it, and I intend to find out. See if you too can find out anything about this Malutica, and then let me know please."

Bill sipped some more wine.

"Another point of interest – my Chief ordered the driver from the fire incident to be released into his personal custody. He is supposedly to be questioned by a team set up by the Chief, but my partner overheard the Chief saying that it is a waste of time to do any questioning because the driver knows nothing. In addition, the Chief stated that he wants to make sure that the driver continues knowing nothing even if it takes making him stupid. According to my partner the Chief also stated that the one they call Butt will never talk; therefore he is not going to be a problem."

Their meals arrived and they ate in silence for a while. The restaurant was busy. Almost all the tables were occupied and the hum of indiscernible chatter interspersed with laughter bounced off the walls.

Bill seemed preoccupied with his thoughts. He looked around the restaurant abstractedly. Then he focused on the restaurant doors, and frowned, before returning his attention to Albert.

"The third guy, I believe they call him Torch, is still in intensive care and he is the one that worries the Chief the most. He is somewhat closer to Butt, and I suppose he will know more about the reasons for the arson. I am of the firm belief that he is going to be killed," he said.

Albert frowned.

"I'll pass on any information I get to you. You do not talk much, do you?" said Bill.

"No," replied Albert, "but I am a very good listener. It's more or less a part of the way I really am, since I am this way in my private life too. It is very interesting that you have so much confidence in me."

"I'm hoping that the confidence will become mutual," Bill said.

They finished eating and enjoyed the remaining wine. Soon the waiter came over to their table.

"Care for another bottle of wine?" he asked.

"Not for me, thank you," Albert replied. "How about you Bill? If I may call you Bill."

"That is my name. And I am sure that you do not mind me calling you Albert," Bill replied.

"No, no more wine for me," Bill said to the waiter.

"How about dessert?" the waiter asked.

"I'll have two scoops of ice cream," Albert replied, "any flavor will do."

"Nothing for me, thank you," Bill replied.

"I noticed that there was no return address on the letters I received, and no indication of the recipient or the sender of the letters. How do you accomplish such effectiveness?" Albert said.

"Well, remember I told you to be on guard in your Agency? I have to do the same, so I only deal with people that I have full confidence in. I sincerely hope you will too. Your life might depend on it." Bill beckoned to the waiter, and then continued, "I am so glad we had this meeting. We will meet somewhere else next time."

Bill paid the bill and left a sizeable tip for the waiter. Both men then rose from their chairs.

"You can go ahead. I have to stop at the restroom," Bill said.

Albert entered the lobby of the restaurant and took a seat in the waiting area, hoping to see Bill leaving. A short time later Bill came into the lobby carrying a take-out order. He had taken off his tie, and his jacket was draped over his hand. He acknowledged Albert with a curt nod and passed by without stopping.

On his way home Albert was deep in thought, What the hell am I getting myself into? Here I am supposedly working to help people and protect their interests, and now I'm faced with secret agent tasks. Now that I have met with Bill, I'm now very deeply involved as his point person. It really seems that everything I've found out so far is intertwined.

26

T he next day Albert asked Nora to join him for lunch. She immediately knew that he wanted to speak with her under private circumstances. She had brought her lunch to work as usual, but she agreed. They left the office and stopped at the nearby hot dog stand where they bought hot dogs and sodas. Then they walked a short distance to the park overlooking a lake and sat down. For a while they munched on their hot dogs and enjoyed the scenery in silence.

"How was your exclusive meeting yesterday? I guess you liked the restaurant?" Nora finally asked.

"The restaurant is a really nice place, and dinner with the Detective was very casual. His name is Bill Hall. He was very forthright. He named you, Blair and Jake as being very trustworthy and having great integrity. He spoke highly of Norm and said that we have a few other good people in the Agency, but he did not name any of those people. He mentioned, just as you had speculated, that the Chief of Police and our Boss have something secretive going on. He is not sure what it is but said that the name Malutica kept coming up and he cannot figure out who or what Malutica really is."

Albert took a bite of his hotdog and chewed for a while, then he swallowed and continued speaking.

"He said our Boss is a very devious person, and that I need to be careful around him. He also said that I should not trust Evin Flek because he is in thick with the Boss."

"Hmmm," said Nora. "Let's see if we can add this up. The Police Chief calls our Boss to find out what, and how much, we know. Our Boss calls you into his office and requests that you brief him on a bi-weekly basis. I think he needs specific information from you to pass on to the Police

Chief."

"Bill was given details of a conversation that one of his staff overheard. Supposedly the Chief of Police has a plan to make the driver involved in the fire incident stupid so that he will be mute. In addition the Police Chief indicated that the guy named Torch is expendable because of what he might know. So Torch might be killed. There definitely appears to be a link between the Chief of Police and the arsonists. Bill also mentioned that something or someone named Malutica is key to the conspiracy between our Boss and the Chief of Police, so we have to get a move on finding out what Malutica is."

"So, what's your impression of Bill Hall?" Nora asked.

"He seems straightforward and dedicated, but he works more like a secret agent than like a detective. Later on I might grow to confide in him, but for now he needs to earn my trust."

Albert sighed.

"We will have to be extra careful based on what we now know because we may be walking on very thin ice. We will continue to have our meetings as usual, but our documents and reports will be edited. For matters of real importance, remember to use the palm of your hand and keep information in your head," he said.

It was time to head back to the office.

"Thanks for coming to lunch," said Albert, as they got up from the park bench. "You walk ahead. I'll keep a good distance between us. We never know who we might run into."

They needn't have feared being seen together. Everyone outside the building was too busy watching and cheering two guys who were fighting over a parking space. It was quite a spectacle. There were more judges and referees than there were fans. Albert found it amusing to see two grown men dressed in office clothes, including ties, in a boxing match in the middle of the workday in a parking lot with so many people cheering and clapping at each punch.

The fighting finally came to an end when the police arrived and broke it up. The two men then hugged each other, shook hands, and bowed to the crowd. At that point people cheered even louder, and the cheers lasted for a long time. Some people even asked the men for autographs.

Albert made his way through the crowd and returned to his office. He was now focused on finding out about Malutica and its connection to, and impact on, the fire incident. I wish I could get another chance to question Butt, he thought, maybe I could pry some information out of him.

Albert frowned. He had a notion that talking to Butt once more would not be very fruitful. Guess I'll have to wait until the one they call Torch comes out of his coma, he thought. He decided to call the hospital to find out if Torch had made any progress toward being out of his coma.

"Torch was found dead in his hospital bed earlier this afternoon," said the doctor.

"Under what circumstances did he die?" Albert asked.

"Suspected poisoning," the doctor replied.

So Bill was right that there was a plan to kill Torch before he could talk, Albert thought.

"Thanks a lot doctor," Albert said.

"You're very welcome Mr. Noble," the doctor replied.

This case is much bigger than I imagined, Albert muttered to himself.

Later that day Albert received another letter. It was delivered in the usual manner, by the same source.

"Wait a minute Norm," Albert said to him in a loud voice. "Who gave you this letter?"

"Somebody who trusts you. Somebody who you can trust. Believe me, you can trust him," Norm replied.

"Thank you very much Norm," said Albert.

Given Norms' response, Albert now associated Norm with Bill. He remembered Bill telling him that he could put his life in Norms' hands. He thought, Bill and Norm must know each other very well, and for a long time too. Maybe somebody might know about their relationship and could tell me more.

Albert placed the letter in his briefcase and decided to call it a day. He decided to read the letter when he got home, when he would be more relaxed.

"You seem taken up with your love letter," Jean said to him. "You haven't put it down since you started reading it."

"I have to memorize some of the contents which might be of great importance to a case I'm working on," Albert replied. "Which reminds me, I have to call Nora. It is important that I meet with her early in the morning."

Albert promptly called Nora and told her that he had received another letter from the Chief of Detectives. He arranged to meet with her the next day in the customer parking lot at the Agency one half hour before work start time.

27

The following day Albert arrived at the Agency very early and drove into the customer parking lot. He was driving Jeans' car to avoid being detected. Nora was already there and he pulled into a parking space about nine cars away from her. He walked over and got into the back of her car.

"Good morning Nora," he said.

"Good morning to you Albert. What is this letter all about?" Nora replied.

"Here, you had better read it yourself," Albert said, handing her the letter. "This is getting to be really bad."

Nora read the letter.

"Well we should not be too surprised about Torch being killed. Neither about the connection between the Police Chief and our Boss," she commented. "I've always had suspicions about Evin, but I also thought he was just playing up to the Boss and taking tales about the office to him."

"It's getting late and we have to go in but before we go, I had a brief talk with Norm when he brought me the letter. While he did not admit it, I think that he is very close to Bill and is the contact person between Bill and I," said Albert. "See you inside, I'll be there soon. I have to destroy this letter first."

The letter had stated that Torch was now dead, the driver had memory loss and was detained by the Chief of Police, and Butt had been given a large sum of money and secretly taken out of town with a stern warning not to return. No one had seen Butt in weeks, the letter stated.

At their meeting that morning, the team decided to give the Boss only the information that was reported in the news media rather than reveal information that would make him suspect that they were aware of his possible involvement in the circumstances related to their investigation.

The holiday weekend was coming up and Blairs' brother was hosting a barbecue party at his home. He had asked Blair to invite a couple of his friends, so Blair invited Nora, Albert and Jake. Blair excluded other Agency staff from his invitation since he saw the party as a good opportunity to discuss their teams' work under more private circumstances.

At the party the team huddled in a corner, away from the other guests.

"I'll try to be very brief," Nora began. "I've found out about Malutica. It is actually a place and not a person. My source in the Title and Records Office told me that it is an Indian reservation about two thousand miles outside of the city. Loop Development, along with some insiders in the Title and Records Office that are loyal to our Boss and the Chief of Police, have been illegally falsifying documents. As a result, a lot of land belonging to the people of Malutica have been stolen. So far Loop Development has acquired about a quarter of the land and they are planning to acquire much more. I also found information related to your instincts about Bill and Norm. Norm is not acting as an agent for Bill. He does things for Bill as a favor. Norm had been a sergeant to Bills' brother Tim while he was in the army and had saved Tims' life when they were together on the combat field. That's where Norm got injured. Ever since that happened Bill and Norm developed a loving, trusting and respectful relationship. Bills' family embraces Norm, and regard him as part of their family."

"Hey guys, today isn't a working day!" Blairs' brother called out to them. "Nothing will be left for you to eat by the time you get through with that project you're discussing!"

Nora and the team ended their discussion.

"Go get a plate and help yourselves," Blairs' brother told them as they approached him. "No waiter is available, so it is self-service and there is enough for seconds."

The food was so good that many people actually returned for seconds. Some people even went back for a third serving.

After dinner everyone enjoyed drinks from the bar and an evening of music and games which included checkers and scrabble. Jean was hailed as the best scrabble player of the evening since she won all the games that she played in. Blair was crowned checkers champion and Jake jokingly accused him of cheating. The party crowd made toasts to the game champions, who were told that they would have to wait until next year to receive their trophies.

Soon the wonderful evening of fun and games came to an end.

"Can we come again next weekend?" Jake asked, while on his way out.

"Sure," he was told. "Next week, and the week after, and the week after…"

"Ok, I'll see you all here again next weekend. Bye for now," he said.

Jean had finally gotten a chance to socialize with Alberts' co-workers and to evaluate how important he was to them. Although she had surmised that the party had been a means for his team to discuss work matters, she was far too impressed with them to feel isolated or left out. She decided that Nora was indeed a remarkable person and that she was thorough and precise, just as Albert had described her to be. She found Jake and Blair to be genuine and very friendly, with a great deal of admiration for Albert.

"So, I guess you did your evaluation of everyone there today?" Albert asked once they were home.

"Yes, everyone but you," she replied with a smile, "and now it's time to evaluate you. I do hope that you are up to it."

Albert had never seen Jean in such a sensual mood. She led in every aspect of their love-making that night.

"I have to do as Jake asked, and have us go to the same

gathering every weekend," Albert whispered in her ear.

Jean smiled and sighed. She gently kissed Albert on his neck.

"Yes, you do that, and you will get the same treatment every time," she replied.

They snuggled together and drifted off to sleep.

28

Wrens' wedding was a week away and the last-minute details were being put in place. Greff had hoped that his wedding would be at the Himda Resort in Trombago, but Wren finally decided that it would be best to have a church wedding in New York in order to accommodate the many guests living there. As such, with no questions asked, Greff had presented Wren with a wedding gift of an all-expenses paid trip to the resort.

It was a typical church wedding, with about two hundred people attending. The ceremony was brief and modest, and the reception was an open-air affair by a large outdoor pool at a hotel. Natures' elements cooperated well for the occasion. The evening sky was perfectly blue, with only traces of white clouds, and at nightfall twinkling stars augmented the candlelight setting. The catering was done in a professional manner, with an excellent variety of dishes. In addition the open bar played a major role in making the reception inviting and care-free.

Greff and Albert, while conversing and enjoying drinks at the far end of the bar, were observing a number of ladies who were trying to grab Grants' undivided attention. It was obvious that they were all attracted to him and that each of them were vying for his personal interest.

Greff casually sauntered over to them and asked for Grant to be excused from the group.

"Those ladies were keenly vying for your undivided attention, you know," Greff said, after he and Grant had walked a few feet away.

"Really? I didn't even realize," Grant replied.

"So, with all these ladies going crazy for you, what plans do you really have in mind?" Greff asked.

"I have to be frank about this. I am not totally ready for

a serious relationship. I've been out on a few dates, some a little more daring than others, but I've made no commitments so nothing has developed so far," Grant replied.

The evening continued with lots of dancing, typical conversations of days gone by and current events, and much enjoyment of the food and drinks. Soon the bride and groom separated from the festivities and departed for their honeymoon in Trombago.

It was a honeymoon to remember forever. Dale fell in love with the beauty of the island and wished she could make Trombago her home. The couple consummated their marriage with a hunger and passion they never realized before. Their beautiful surroundings, coupled with the tranquility and relaxation they enjoyed, allowed them to replenish their appetite for love-making each day.

29

When Albert awoke on Monday morning, he moaned. It seemed that the weekend had been too short. He looked over at Jean and smiled. She looked beautiful, even though she was just waking up.

"I wish I did not have to go to work today," he said to Jean.

"You can stay home. You've earned a day or two off from work. We could stay in bed and make love all day," Jean replied.

"I must say, that is a very good idea," Albert responded with a smile.

Albert called the Agency and spoke with Nora.

"Just be sure that you come in to work tomorrow," Nora told him. "Something important has come up."

"Okay, I'll be there," Albert replied, and hung up the phone.

"What's wrong?" Jean inquired. "Do you have to go to work?"

"Seems like something came up, but it can wait until tomorrow, because for today nothing is going to come between our making love," Albert replied. He pulled Jean into his arms and kissed her passionately.

Their lovemaking was sensual and steamy. At the end they were both spent. Afterwards Albert gazed into Jeans' beautiful brown eyes and smiled.

"You are becoming a real terror in bed lately. What are you feeding on?" he teased.

"I've been feeding on my love for you, of which I cannot get enough," Jean replied.

The following day Albert was the first of the team members to arrive at the Agency. Soon after, Nora arrived.

"How was your day yesterday? You look well-rested," she said to him.

"I did the best I could," Albert replied. "So, what's new?"

Nora had written a brief note. She handed it to him. It explained that her friend at the Title and Records Office had told her that an agency in Malutica had some vital information of great value to the investigation.

"They require someone from our Agency to come in person, as some guarantees have to be made before they can release any information," Nora elaborated. "I think that they are a bit cautious and are taking safeguards. Somehow they heard a little about you and think that you would work on their behalf."

"Do I sense some urgency in this matter?" Albert asked.

"No, not really," Nora replied. "If you left here in two weeks or so, that would be fine. I'm sure you will have to discuss it with Jean before making a decision to go there."

Later that night, over dinner with Jean, Albert mentioned the prospect of taking a trip to Malutica. Jean was at first apprehensive but reasoned that such a trip fell within his job description and so she resigned herself to the fact that it would only be for a short time. As such, the trip to Malutica was planned for the following weekend. They both decided that Albert would travel by car in order for him to get familiar with the geography and surrounding townships. Travel time was estimated at eleven to twelve hours.

30

Nora had chosen Nelson, an employee in the transportation section of the Agency, as Alberts' designated driver. He was known to be an efficient and reliable driver. With a chuckle, Nora had described Nelson as quite a ladies' man with a reputation of knowing how to make the ladies happy.

It was a bright sunny Saturday morning when Nelson arrived at Alberts' home. He was on time and seemed eager about going on the trip. Jean had packed a basket with fried chicken and sandwiches, and a cooler with a couple of beers and some fruit punch. She knew that Albert loved her fried chicken and would enjoy it during the trip. On his way out the door, Albert embraced her.

"I love you," he whispered in her ear, before giving her a passionate kiss.

"Hurry back," Jean replied. "I love you too."

"Do you have a map to guide us?" Albert asked Nelson, as he climbed into the car.

"Sure, and I have worked out how many stops we might be making for gas, rest, and possible emergencies," Nelson replied.

"You seem to be on top of everything," Albert responded.

"Well, I always try to plan ahead. It makes things a little easier," said Nelson.

After driving for two hours, listening to music, and chatting about the Agency and the weather, the men were now approaching some breathtaking country and hillside views.

"This reminds me so much of my birthplace," Albert said.

"Where were you born?" Nelson asked.

"On the island of Trombago," Albert replied.

"I've never been outside of this country. As a matter of fact, I've never even been on a helicopter ride," Nelson said.

"You should visit Trombago sometime. I could arrange for you to stay with my parents," Albert suggested.

"That's a good idea. Thanks for offering to do that. Well, here we go, our first stop," said Nelson, while turning the car into a gas station.

The men filled up the gas tank, used the restroom, and then relaxed in the car where they enjoyed some of the treats that Jean had prepared.

"This is very good. It is very tasty," said Nelson. "You have a very good wife. How long have you been married?"

"Just about two years now," Albert replied. "How about you? Do you have a family?"

"I was married, but my wife stepped out on me," Nelson replied. "It's a long and sad story." Nelson changed the subject. "Some people in the Agency refer to you as Digger. Is that a nickname?"

"That's what they call me? I was not aware of that. I wonder why," said Albert.

"Some people in the Agency say that you are a very honest person, and that you are too straight and always digging for truth. They say that you will not stop until you find out the truth, so I guess that is why they gave you the name Digger," said Nelson.

"It's the first I'm hearing of this," Albert responded. "Should I take that as a compliment?"

"You should! You're highly respected by most for being the way you are, even though some think that you are too disciplined and precise," said Nelson.

"That is just the way I was brought up to be – honest and fair. I guess it is a family trait," said Albert.

"Well, let's get going," said Nelson. "We still have a long way to go. I hope our next stop will be at the motel, but I think we may have to make one more stop before actually getting there."

"Let me take over driving at the next stop. By then you should be dog tired," said Albert.

"I doubt that I will be really tired, but I accept your offer," Nelson replied.

After driving for another two hours, they decided to stop at a small gas station with a grocery store facing the only two gas pumps. The store had an assortment of snacks and sandwiches, as well as coffee, cold drinks and doughnuts. There were two chairs leaning against the front wall of the small store. Albert and Nelson rested on the chairs for several minutes, enjoying the quietness of the small town.

"Well, here you go boss," said Nelson, handing the car keys to Albert. "You're now the pilot."

The men continued on their journey, enjoying the beauty of the surrounding countryside in silence. Although the scenery was invigorating, it was also relaxing to the extent that one could easily fall asleep. Nelson sensed the feeling that the scenery would precipitate and broke the silence, in an effort to prevent himself from falling asleep.

"How is it that you did not ask why my wife skipped out on me? Is it that you already know?" he asked.

"No, I do not know. I figured that if you wanted me to know, you would tell me. I figured that maybe it is a private matter," Albert replied.

"Oh no, not really. Quite a few people know the facts. I am totally to be blamed. I have a tendency to run around quite a lot. Somehow it's hard for me to resist a pretty woman. I'm sure you've heard something about my reputation with the ladies?" asked Nelson.

"As a matter of fact, I have never heard anything specific regarding your life until now. But based on what you're telling me, I must say that you seem to live an exciting life," said Albert.

"Well that was my undoing. My wife caught me more than once. She got tired of my escapades, and she finally left," Nelson explained.

"And you haven't changed?" Albert asked.

"Oh no. In fact, I've gotten a little worse," Nelson replied with a wry smile. "I now feel free, and don't have to look behind me. So how about you? You must have had some good times with the ladies."

"Not like you, I'm sure," said Albert. "A few dates in college. Some I thought would develop into something serious, but they never did. Since I got married, I've remained faithful to my wife."

They were driving through a town with a small marina and a few houses that were one to two acres apart.

"Aren't these people lonely, living like this?" Albert remarked.

"Not really," Nelson responded. "These are rich ass people, with lots of money to spare. They come here once or maybe twice each month to relax, party, and fish. It's their way of easing stress and getting away from the crowded city."

Soon they were driving by several acres of vacant land. Albert began speculating, Look at all this vacant land lying here. I wonder why someone would want to take away this land from the Indians….

Nelson, who had been looking at the map, suddenly broke into Alberts' thoughts.

"We should be at the motel very soon," he said.

Sure enough, within minutes, they saw a sign. It read: Stay Easy Motel – 20 miles ahead.

"We can stay there tonight and leave early tomorrow morning when we are well rested and fresh," Nelson said.

"That's a damn good idea. I'm all for it," Albert replied.

31

When they entered the Stay Easy Motel they saw two clerks behind the counter – one seemed to be assigned to check in guests, and the other appeared to be a bell boy.

"How long are you staying?" the check-in clerk asked.

"Overnight," Albert replied.

"Separate rooms?" the clerk asked.

"No, but separate beds," said Albert.

"That will be twenty-five dollars, payable in advance," the clerk said.

"Sure, here you go," said Albert, handing him the money.

Just then a man emerged through a door from what seemed to be an office behind the counter.

"Welcome to the Stay Easy Motel gentlemen," he said to them. "I'm the manager Don Scott. We will endeavor to make your stay as comfortable as possible. There is a diner, a gift shop, an ice cream and soda shop, and a bar just over on the other side of the motel. They are just a short walk away. So where are you guys heading?"

"Malutica," Nelson replied. "How far away is that?"

"About three hours away, but there is nothing but Indians there," said Don. "Anybody in particular you're going to see?"

"Just an army buddy we haven't seen in years," Albert replied.

The bell boy escorted them to their room. Albert and Nelson decided not to unpack; instead they showered, selected a change of clothing, and headed to the diner for dinner.

The diner was quaint and clean. Albert chose fish with

rice pilaf and Nelson selected steak with baked potatoes. The men ordered beer but were told that the diner was not allowed to sell strong drinks, since that would be in competition with the bar. The waitress offered them non-alcoholic wine.

"Let's have a bottle of that please," said Albert. "White."

As soon as the wine arrived, Nelson poured some into their glasses and immediately drank a full glass as though he was dehydrated.

"How is it?" Albert asked him.

"Not bad, but I still would prefer beer," Nelson replied. "Let's go check out the bar when we are done."

The men finished eating and walked a short distance to the cozy little bar. There were a few small tables set up with chairs along the far side of the entrance, and the bar itself was situated near to the entrance. It had a long counter with several bar stools where Albert suspected that the regulars sat.

Albert and Nelson sat at the counter and were greeted by a pleasant middle-aged woman. She enjoyed a couple of beers with them and shared the fact that she was the owner of the bar, While they chatted Nelson made advances to her and he would have been successful at having her agree to spend the night with him, but Albert reminded him that they would be leaving the motel early in the morning.

Meanwhile, during the time that Albert and Nelson were away from the motel, Don Scott had looked over the vehicle they came in, noted the vehicle number and registration details, and called the Police Chief. Don was a member of the group of "land grabbers" and his mission was to inform the Police Chief about any person or persons asking about Malutica. The Police Chief had then called Alberts' boss to find out what Albert would be doing in Malutica.

"I know nothing about that. I did not even know that he was out of the city. Let me get in touch with Flek and get back to you," Peter said to the Police Chief.

Peter immediately called Flek.

"Flek here, what can I do for you?"

"Hey Flek. It's Peter. Tell me, what do you know about Albert going to Malutica in Agency Vehicle #S602?"

"I had no idea that he was going there," Flek replied.

"Well find out about it fast and get back to me. This guy is after something, and you can bet on it that he will bring us all down if he can associate us with Malutica!" Peter exclaimed.

Flek had always had a good relationship with the manager in the Transportation section of the Agency. Because of this, he was able to call him even though it was Saturday evening.

"Hey Bob, do you know anything about Vehicle #S602 being used in any way?"

"Yes, I do," Bob replied. "Nelson is assigned to it for six days."

"Do you know where he is going?" Flek asked.

"No, but he said it was a long ride and that Sally was upset that he was going away. She wanted him to be with her this weekend," Bob replied.

"Thanks a lot Bob. You've been a great help," Flek said.

Sally was Fleks' secretary and lover. She was also desperately in love with Nelson and would demand his attention every so often. She was on the phone when Flek called her, but he kept calling intermittently until she finally accepted his call.

"Hey Sally, can you meet me at Multys Café in an hour?" he asked her. "It's very important."

Sally arrived at the café fifteen minutes late. She was dressed as though she expected to have an evening out with Flek.

"Would you like to share a drink?" Flek asked her.

"Yes, wine please," she replied.

"So, what is so important that you want to see me about tonight?" Sally asked him.

"You sure look great," Flek said to her. His eyes had

stopped at her bosom. Then he looked up into her face. "Can you stay late?"

"Sure, I have no one to go home to," Sally replied.

"Why is that?" Flek asked. "I thought you and Nelson…."

"Oh him," Sally interjected. "He has gone to some place called Mantula."

"Malutica?" Flek asked her.

"Yes. With that Albert guy. For the weekend. They must be homosexual or something," Sally said with exasperation.

"Why are they going there?" Flek asked.

"He did not say. But I think Albert is going to meet with someone there," Sally said.

"Ok. Let's finish up here and then spend the rest of the evening together. I'll be right back," Flek replied.

Flek went to a private phone booth and called Peter.

"Flek here," he said when Peter answered.

"Yes Evin, what have you got for me?" Peter asked.

"I confirmed that Albert is heading to Malutica. He is being driven by Nelson and is using company Vehicle #S602. I do not know exactly why he is going there, but he is going to see someone. I don't know who though," Flek replied.

"Good work," Peter said. "We've got to stop that bastard somehow. He is digging too deep into matters that do not concern him. Thanks again."

Flek returned to the table, paid the bill, and left the restaurant with Sally.

After speaking with Flek, Peter immediately called the Police Chief.

"Peter here," he spoke into the receiver.

"Yes Peter, what have you got for me?" the Police Chief asked him.

"Well I have confirmation that this guy Albert is indeed heading for Malutica. He is going there to see someone. Who it is and for what reason, I do not know; but knowing this guy, he can make things really bad for us. We've got to stop him somehow," Peter said.

"When Don called and told me about Agency Vehicle #S602, I thought it was being used by you or Flek. But when he told me the name of the person who booked the room I became suspicious, and that is why I decided to call you," said the Police Chief.

"Oh no, I would have informed you if either myself or Flek were going to Malutica," said Peter. "Anyway, regardless of that, this guy has got to be stopped."

"I promise you, he won't be keeping that appointment," said the Police Chief. "Not if I can help it."

When the Police Chief hung up he called his pilot and sidekick and instructed him to have the helicopter ready for take-off. He then called Don to get a full description of the vehicle that Albert and Nelson were using.

"It is white, with #S602 printed in upper case, in red ink, on the top and on the sides of it," Don explained. "There is no way you can miss it."

"Ok. I'll be at the Lodge. Call me the minute they leave," the Police Chief instructed. "It is very important that we prevent these guys from ever reaching Malutica."

The Police Chief, his partner Wally, and his pilot Barry departed for the Lodge. The Lodge was a two-cabin structure situated at the border of Malutica and was the designated meeting place for the Police Chief and his special group of associates.

Meanwhile, Albert and Nelson had returned to their room at the Stay Easy Motel with a couple of beers and had been playing cards. Soon they decided to call it a day and retired for the night.

32

The next morning Nelson was the first to awaken. He felt well-rested and energized, and immediately began thinking about a cup of coffee. He hopped out of bed and nudged Albert.

"Hey man. Time for us to get ready and get on the road," he said to him.

The men refreshed themselves, got dressed, packed, and headed for the front desk. When they got there, they found Don sitting alone behind the counter.

"How was your stay gentlemen?" he asked.

"Very good," Albert replied. "Where can we get breakfast?"

"The diner does not open until nine, but there is coffee, doughnuts and deli sandwiches at the gas station about ten minutes down the road," Don replied.

"Thank you," said Albert. "We will see you on the way back."

"Drive safely, and I look forward to seeing you again soon," Don said. "Thanks for stopping at the Stay Easy Motel."

Nelson assumed his position around the wheel and soon they were at the gas station. They filled the gas tank and had coffee, sandwiches, and a couple of doughnuts. Albert ordered coffee to go and paid the bill.

"How far is it to Malutica?" Nelson asked the cashier.

"Oh, about two or three hours," the cashier replied.

"I'm heading to Malutica," a man who was standing in line chimed in. "Would you be kind enough to give me a ride? My transportation is hours away from here. Rather than wait for it, I'd just cancel it."

Nelson looked over at Albert, seeking his permission. After a brief pause, they both agreed to give the man a ride.

"He might be able to help us," Albert whispered.

Albert took the documents related to the vehicle from the glove compartment, and his briefcase from the front section, and invited the stranger to sit in the front seat. It was his way of being cautious.

"I'm Nelson, and the gentleman sitting in the back is Albert," Nelson said, as he settled into the drivers' seat.

"Glad to meet you both. I'm Manny. I live on the reservation. My father lives here in town and I try to visit him as often as I possibly can. My mother died a few years ago and because of that he moved away from the reservation to overcome the memory of her passing," said Manny. "So, are you going to see anyone in particular in Malutica?"

"An old army buddy of ours," Nelson replied.

"Do you know Lebron?" Albert chimed in.

"Sure, everybody knows Lebron. He is one of the most educated and respected men on the reservation. He, like me, is half-Indian. His father and my father are very close friends. LeBron had moved away with his family when he was in his early teens. After he completed his education, he came right back to Malutica to try and make things better for our people. He has been with us ever since," said Manny. "He has done some positive things in Malutica, with the promise of more to come."

Albert thought, It was a good idea to give Manny a ride after all. He does seem to be genuine, and he might be able to point us in the right direction.

They were almost two hours into their journey when they heard a helicopter above them.

"It's just the police circling around," Manny said.

Those were the last words he spoke. The helicopter hovered in front of the vehicle and a barrage of bullets was discharged at them.

Nelson quickly maneuvered the vehicle into a thicket. When he looked over at Manny he saw that he was slumped against the door. He was bleeding from his head.

"Albert!" Nelson shouted. "Are you okay!"

"Yes. Yes. I'm okay!" Albert replied. He leaned over the headrest and checked Manny. "Oh God Nelson, I think he is dead!"

Nelson skillfully steered the car through the thicket until he got to a dense section where he slowed down to less than five miles per hour.

"Get the hell out Albert! Now! I'll try to lose them!"

Albert did not think twice. He immediately opened the door and jumped over an embankment used as a breakfront to prevent soil erosion. He then climbed a tree in order to see how Nelson was making out.

Albert could see the vehicle swerving along the path through the trees, then it reached a clearing. The helicopter was now approaching it from the front as it entered the clearing. Another barrage of bullets hit it from every angle. Suddenly the vehicle swerved erratically and continued a short distance before coming to a stop at the edge of a steep ravine.

The helicopter landed and two men came out. They walked up to the vehicle, fired a number of shots into the two bodies inside it, then they pushed it over the edge into the river below.

Albert was expecting to hear an explosion, but all he heard was the sound of the vehicle hitting against rocks and stones. He watched as the men climbed back into the helicopter and, as the helicopter flew above him, he got a good look at the numbers and letters that were imprinted on it. However, he was not able to clearly see who the men were.

After a few minutes Albert decided it was safe to get down from the tree. He was shaking. He was in a state of shock over what had happened. He didn't realize that there was a rotted tree branch lying on the ground beneath the tree. He stepped on it, lost his balance, fell, and hit his head on a rock. He immediately lost consciousness.

It was several hours before Albert was accidentally found. A boy and his sister were enjoying their afternoon horseback ride when they stumbled on him lying on the ground. They lifted his eyelids, listened for his heartbeat, and realized that he was alive. Soon they saw the wound on his head. They proceeded to wash the wound with water from their canteen. The boy wet his bandana and tied it around Alberts' head. Then he moistened Alberts' lips with some of the water.

"Go get Daddy," he said to his sister. "He will know what to do."

"It'll take too much time to go there and come back," his sister replied. "Let's take him. It'll be much quicker."

Together they heaved Albert on to the boys' horse and slowly rode back to the reservation.

"I will take him to our house. You run and get Daddy," the boy said.

The moment Lebron got to his house and saw Albert, he got on the phone.

"Preston, could you come over here right away and bring your instruments, medicines, and medical aids? And, please, come alone."

Lebron removed the blood-soaked bandana from Alberts' head and proceeded to clean his wound. He soaked a cotton ball with rubbing alcohol and held it under Alberts' nose, since he did not have any smelling salts. Albert remained unresponsive. Lebron intermittently applied rubbing alcohol to Alberts' head and neck until Preston arrived.

When Preston arrived, he immediately stripped Albert down to his underwear.

"He is alive for sure," he said to Lebron. "A broken collar bone, two broken ribs, and a mild coma from hitting his head. He should be coming out of the coma over the next several hours. But sadly, he will suffer from amnesia. It will be a long time before he remembers what happened to him, or even remembers his past for that matter."

Preston proceeded to apply bandages to Alberts' body to support his broken bones and keep them in place. Then he stitched the wound on his head and secured the stitches with a thick bandage around his head. While he was doing that Lebron retrieved Alberts' wallet from his pant pocket. His Agency badge with his identification number and his drivers' license were still inside.

"Preston, take a look at this!" he exclaimed. "He is the person we have been waiting for to have the meeting. He is Albert Noble from the Agency. I wonder what the hell happened here…"

"Manzi, Dori, where did you find this man?" Lebron asked his children.

"Dori and I rode for maybe an hour after we set out from the reservation," Manzi replied.

"Was he alone?" asked Lebron.

"Yes, but it seems as if there was an accident. There was some smoke coming from the ravine near to where we found him. We were so taken up with him, we forgot to tell you about it," said Manzi.

"Ok, do not say a word about this to anyone. And I mean anyone. Can I trust you all on this?" Lebron said.

"Yes," they replied in unison.

"Good. Now come show me where you found him," Lebron said.

"Lebron, I have to get back to the clinic," Preston interjected. "There is a patient that I must see today."

"Sure Preston, but you will check on him regularly for me, won't you?" Lebron asked.

"Definitely. You can count on me as always. I've given him a shot so he will be sleeping for a while," Preston replied.

Preston packed his bag and both men walked to the door.

"Thank you for coming Preston. You might just have saved his life," Lebron said.

"Oh no, it was Manzi and Dori who saved his life. If

they had not used their instincts and acted in the manner that they did, he would not be alive. But I will be back to see him later," replied Preston.

"Come along Manzi, let's go have a look at the place where you found him," said Lebron. "Dori, please stay here until your mom gets home. She should be home any minute now. Explain to her what happened and let her know that we will be back as soon as possible."

"Yes dad," Dori replied.

33

anzi took his father to the location where he and
Dori had found Albert. They went by horseback
to prevent suspicion and to allow them to easily
backtrack within the surrounding areas. When Lebron
backtracked a couple hundred feet from the spot where
Albert had been found, he noticed tire marks entering the
thicket from the direction of the road. He followed the path
of the tire marks through the thicket until he reached the
clearing. There he saw indications that the vehicle had
swerved after it had entered the clearing, before making an
erratic turn towards the ravine.

Lebron and Manzi dismounted and followed the tire
marks to the edge of the ravine. Some of the rocks at the
edge had broken off, and there were tire marks and engine
oil on the remaining rocks. Lebron looked around. He
noticed a burnt section in the clearing and surmised that it
must have been caused by a helicopter. He wanted to
evaluate his assessment, but before that he wanted to take a
look inside the ravine itself. He hesitated. The ravine was
steep, and a long way down from ground level. Nothing
could survive a fall down there, he thought, and besides,
there were piranhas down there.

Lebron turned and looked back toward the clearing. It
was then that he saw shells, from bullets, lying on the
ground. He gathered a few of them and decided to retrace
his steps to see if there was anything else that he had missed
earlier.

He and Manzi were on their way back to the spot where
Albert had been found when Manzi suddenly stopped and
pointed to some trees with holes in the trunks.

"Look Dad!" he exclaimed.

Lebron nodded.

"I see," he said. "Those are bullet holes. I'm sure we will find a lot more before long."

As they walked around, Lebrons' suspicions were confirmed. Many of the surrounding tree trunks had bullet holes, and some had bullets in them.

"I'll only take a few of the bullets from the ground, as they are considered evidence," Lebron said.

When they got back to the spot where Albert had been found Lebron noticed broken tree branches, as well as blood on a big rock, below the tree. A few feet away he found Alberts' briefcase.

Lebron and Manzi followed the tire tracks back to the road and noticed many more bullets and shells scattered across the ground.

"I would say that the bullets were fired from above, based on the angle that they bored into the tree trunks. It is now clear that the bullets were fired from a helicopter. I believe murder was the motive here. Manzi, be sure to remember the things I've described. They could be of great value to you some day," said Lebron.

"Sure Dad. I won't forget," Manzi replied.

"Let us put a heavy layer of dirt over the rock with the blood on it. I wouldn't want anyone to find out about the man you found. Then let me get a few more of the bullets before we head for home," said Lebron.

When he got home Lebron found his wife eagerly waiting to find out what happened. He explained to her that Albert had come to help the people of Malutica with the preservation of their land.

"It seems that he, and those with him, were attacked on the way here. Somehow he survived the attack, and Manzi and Dori found him. We can't keep him here for too long though. I'll have to get him to a safe place as his life may be in danger. At some point the accident will be reported to the police, and they will go to the scene and try to find the vehicle and determine if there are any casualties," said Lebron.

Later that day the fire department received a report that smoke was coming from the ravine. Shortly afterwards two fire trucks, an ambulance, and a police car with two officers arrived at the scene. They immediately cordoned off the area.

"What happened?" a curious onlooker asked one of the policemen as he walked by.

"Looks like some drunken fool must have driven his car over the embankment to his certain death below," the policeman replied. "It is going to be very difficult to get down there, but a special team is on their way here. If it is not too dark, and not too dangerous, they can try to get down there when they arrive. Otherwise they will have to come back tomorrow morning."

"It is so sad when things like this happen," said the onlooker.

Another onlooker approached them.

"Some people are saying that there are a lot of piranhas down there in the water, and that by the time your men get here they will only find bones and car parts," he interjected.

Soon the special team arrived. They assessed the situation and determined that, since it was getting dark, it would be too dangerous to even attempt to go down into the ravine.

The news was broadcast on all airways that night and people in the area were anxious to know more about the incident. As a result, there was a large crowd waiting at the scene when the special team arrived there early the following morning. Lebron stood in the midst of the crowd. He had decided that he would follow all developments on the incident.

A team of divers and wreckage retrieving experts descended the steep ravine. When they got to the bottom one of them reported to their lead who was stationed at the embankment.

"This is going to be a very difficult job. There are a lot of flesh-eating fish swimming around," he said.

It took considerable patience and genius to locate and retrieve parts of the wreckage from the ravine. The onlookers watched as car parts were hoisted to the land above the ravine and immediately secured and taken away to be analyzed. Then a crumpled mass of debris, weed, dirt, metal, stones and other indistinguishable items were hoisted to the land. This mass also appeared to contain human body parts and personal belongings. Several onlookers gasped when they saw what appeared to be the bone of an arm sticking out of the thick black net. The entire net was bagged and tagged for review by the medical examiners' office.

After many hours of patient, consistent and careful work, the dive team safely completed what at first appeared to be a hopeless task. When pressed by reporters at the scene, the police officer could not provide any information.

"The car parts and all evidence have been submitted for examination. There is nothing more I can tell you until the examiners' report is released to us," said the officer.

The following day, when the vehicle was identified, the Agency was notified. Nora was extremely surprised and felt a bit responsible since she had selected both men for the mission. However, she was also suspicious.

"Nelson was known to be a very competent and reliable driver," she said in a meeting with the team, "so I firmly believe that something must have happened, other than just a car accident."

Blair immediately volunteered to take a trip to Malutica to conduct an investigation. Nora granted him permission and recommended associates from the Agency for him to travel with. She also provided him with the names of those he should see once he arrived there.

"Travel by private car," she instructed him, "and be sure to call me right away with anything you find out. The Agency has to notify Albert and Nelsons' relatives and the most up to date information I have to give to them, the better."

34

Blair and his team arrived at the medical examiners' office in Malutica in the middle of the examination. They were told that they had to wait until it was complete in order to get any information. Blair asked if he could sit in on the examination procedure, and his request was denied. Blair then asked to be taken to the scene of the accident. He was directed to the police officer in charge of the investigation who assigned a young, but eager and curious, officer to escort him and his team to the scene. This young officer had his own opinion about what had happened and felt fortunate to have been selected to escort Blair and his team to the scene.

When they arrived at the location the officer drove up to where the vehicle had gone over the embankment into the ravine, and they got out and looked over the edge.

"My God!" exclaimed Blair. "Nothing could survive this!"

"It gets worse," said the young officer. "It is infested with piranhas down there. The rescue effort yielded only bones, personal belongings, and parts of the vehicles' interior."

Webb, a member of Blairs team, listened intently as the young officer spoke. He immediately liked him.

"You seem to have a fair amount of knowledge about this incident, and I guess you may also have formed an opinion about what really happened here," he said to him. "By the way, I am Webb, he is Blair, and that's Phil over there."

"Pleased to meet you Sirs. I am Jonas. Everybody calls me Jo and, yes sir, I do have my own opinion about what happened here." He shook his head solemnly and continued. "I think this was no accident. I noticed some bullet holes in the vehicle parts when they brought them up from the ravine."

Jonas pointed to skid marks on the ground to the left of them.

"These skid marks show the angle that the vehicle hit the embankment. Based on this angle, the vehicle could not have gone over the embankment unless it was pushed," he said.

Phil focused on the skid marks and the tire tracks leading up to the embankment.

"Let us follow these tire tracks and see where they lead us," he suggested.

The tracks were broken and very faint in some areas, but there was still an accurate trail to follow. After what seemed like a very long walk they noticed a separate set of tire marks which originated from the direction of the road. Those tracks continued towards the thicket.

"Here is another set of tracks, apparently made with the same tires. Is there time to backtrack along two tracks?" Blair asked.

"Sure. Let's try to find as much evidence as we can while we are here. Evidence might not be here tomorrow," Jonas replied.

The men followed the tracks leading from the road towards the thicket.

"Why would they enter the thicket from the road if they were not avoiding something?" Webb remarked.

"This could be your answer. Look at all these bullet holes," Jonas replied, pointing at the trees around them.

"And there are shells all over the ground," Phil chimed in.

"Let us gather as much of them as possible. They may lead us somewhere or, for that matter, to someone," Blair said.

The men continued to follow the tracks leading towards the thicket. As they walked, they noticed more bullet holes and more spent shells. Then they walked through the thicket to the clearing at the other end and looked around. Blairs' attention was drawn to a burnt section of the clearing not too far from where they had exited the thicket. The men walked over to the spot and noticed where it appeared to have been trampled on.

"Perhaps onlookers, who had probably gathered at the time of discovery, stood here," Blair surmised. "Nonetheless I think the burn was caused by a helicopter."

The men all agreed. They then examined the bullet holes in the trunks of the trees surrounding the clearing and noticed the angle of the bullet marks.

"These bullet marks indicate that the shots were fired from a helicopter," said Jonas.

"Did the police officers on the scene gather evidence from the surroundings?" Blair asked.

"Not really," Jonas replied. "They listed the incident as a car accident and left it at that."

"I would imagine that they might think differently after they get the Medical Examiners' report," said Webb.

"Let's go back over to the thicket and follow the tire tracks from there," Phil said.

The men returned to the location where they had exited the thicket. As they followed the tracks leading away from the thicket they noticed that the tire marks twisted and turned as though the driver had lost control of the vehicle.

"This makes sense," said Blair. "Based on the spent shells on the ground and the angle of the bullet holes in the tree trunks, it seems to me that someone in the helicopter shot at the vehicle as soon as it came out of the thicket. Then the driver lost control."

They continued to follow the tracks until they arrived at the edge of the ravine once more.

"Well, this was definitely no accident," Jonas muttered. "The officers assigned to this incident have overlooked a lot of things here."

"Jonas, are you married?" Blair asked him.

"No sir," Jonas replied.

"Any girlfriend?" Blair asked.

"Yes and no," Jonas answered.

"Which one is it?" Blair asked.

"I have a girlfriend but it is always an on and off situation, so I'm still unsure," Jonas replied.

"How would you like to join our team?" Blair asked him. "The pay is very good, and you can move up quickly. You already seem to like this line of investigative work, and you have a knack for it. We will be here for another week. You can think about it and, if you decide to, we can assist you with the application and all your arrangements and you can come back to the city with us. But I have to insist that you do not say one word about this discussion, or about what we discovered here today, to anyone. Don't even mention what our suspicions are. We could be dealing with something very serious and a lot of proof is going to be needed. Let us see what the medical examiner and the officers assigned to the case conclude."

"Yes sir, you can depend on me to keep quiet about what we suspect here. The police precinct here is not what it used to be. There are some people who think this situation means that some drunk got himself killed in a stupid car accident and there should be no more investigation. As such they think that the incident should be marked with that conclusion, and that should be the end of it," Jonas said. "I am certainly going to think over your proposal and let you know in a couple of days. It might just be the best thing that could happen to me as I am growing weary of some of the things that are going on around my precinct."

35

The next day Blair was granted permission to inspect the recovered car parts. Just as Jonas had said, there were bullet holes in some of them. He was fortunate to find a couple of bullets that no one appeared to have discovered, and he left them in the wreckage since he had already retrieved some from the location of the incident. He thought, what unprofessional work these police officers did. He wondered about the condition of the personal artifacts that they had removed from the wreckage.

Blair decided to go to Lebrons' office. Nora had told him that Lebron would be his contact person, but he was not sure that Lebron would see him without an appointment. He took the trip anyway, and when he arrived he asked the receptionist if Lebron was available.

"Mr. Lebron is out to lunch," the receptionist replied. "He'll be back in another half hour or so. Can anyone else assist you?"

"No, thank you. I have to see him personally. I don't mind waiting," Blair replied.

Blair pulled a magazine from the rack in the waiting area and took a seat. After he sat down, he noticed a newspaper on the center table in front of him. The front of the newspaper displayed a picture of the rescue workers at the ravine with the caption "Car Accident at the Border of Malutica – Artifacts Retrieved from Ravine." Blair picked up the newspaper and read the details. It didn't tell him anything that he didn't already know – vehicle was a total wreck, body or bodies were eaten by piranhas, bones from bodies were being examined by the medical examiner. He flipped through the newspaper lazily, reading sections of articles and glancing at the advertisements. Soon he heard the receptionist speaking in a low tone.

"Mr. Lebron, that gentleman is here to see you," she said.

Blair did not look up and pretended that he did not hear her. He continued flipping the pages of the newspaper. Then he looked up when Lebron spoke to him.

"I am Lebron. Can I help you?"

Lebron had walked over to Blair and was standing directly in front of him.

"I am Blair from the Agency," Blair replied. He pulled out his Agency ID and showed it to Lebron. "Can I talk with you privately?"

"Sure, what about?" Lebron asked.

"Let's go outdoors. My car is right outside the door. We can sit in it while we talk," Blair replied.

The men walked outside and got into Blairs' car.

"I believe you have been following details of the accident closely?" Lebron asked him.

"Yes, and with a lot of interest. Albert Noble, who had an appointment to meet with you, was one of the individuals traveling in that vehicle and from the most recent accounts, he died tragically. I feel a great loss, not just because he was a good man and friend, but because the Agency was expecting a lot to be accomplished from his meeting with you."

"I had waited for his arrival for hours and thought that he must have been delayed or had a change of plans," said Lebron. "I called Nora the day after he was expected, and she told me that he had in fact left the city in time to make the appointment with me. Then I heard about the accident and suspected that it might be the vehicle that Albert was traveling in, but I was waiting for my suspicions to be confirmed by your Agency. How many people in your office knew that he was coming to Malutica?"

"Only the three of us on our team knew," Blair replied.

"Can you think of anyone else that might have found out?" Lebron asked.

"What is this? You suspect our team of some

wrongdoing?" Blair retorted.

"No. I am just looking at all angles. We believe that this was no accident, and that he was deliberately prevented from making it to Malutica," Lebron responded.

"It is only fair to let you know that we have a group of sincere, dedicated, and devoted people working on our team at the Agency. To think that anyone of us would do harm, especially to Albert, is ridiculous," Blair replied.

Lebron considered telling Blair that Albert was alive but decided not to do so as yet. He thought it best to wait awhile in order to ensure Alberts safety, as well as to give himself time to confirm his suspicions.

"So, where do we go from here?" he asked Blair.

"We wait for the police investigation and identification process to be completed, and then take it from there. But when your suspicions, which I have to admit are now mine, are proven correct you can rest assured that our Agency will get to the bottom of this," Blair replied. "I will be returning to the city in about a week, or as soon as I have all the information and reports related to this tragedy. We can meet again before I leave if there is any new information you have about the incident. By the way, what about the information relevant to the meeting that you were to have had with Albert? I look forward to taking that back with me."

"I will gladly provide that to you," Lebron replied. "I will get it for you now."

Lebron went inside his office, returned with a large envelope, and handed it to Blair.

"You will find the names of some people in your Agency mentioned on these documents, but rest assured, everything there is all based on facts. Please sign this confidentiality agreement and these disclosures for my records."

"For some time now our team has been suspicious about some of the people in our Agency, as well as about their affiliations. Thank you for helping us with this case," Blair replied as he signed the documents.

36

A week later Blair and his team departed for home. They had accomplished a lot in a short time and were eager to meet with their other team members to review the results of their visit to Malutica. Jonas was travelling with them. The young officer had eagerly and quickly completed the job application and finalized all necessary arrangements in order to make the trip with them.

During the trip the men evaluated the new information they had and debated some of the details. They all agreed that the local police had been inefficient in their work, but they were satisfied that the new information they had would help them in their investigation.

When they arrived in the city Blair drove directly to the Agency. Nora was surprised to see them and insisted that they should go home and report to work in a day or two.

"I thought it best to drop off this envelope that I received from Lebron," Blair explained. "After receiving it I tucked it away safely in my briefcase. I have not looked at the contents."

"Thank you. This probably contains much of the information that Albert was to have obtained," she said. She looked over at Jonas.

"Who is this gentleman?" she asked.

"This is Jonas," Blair replied. "He has been more helpful to us than the officers responsible for investigating the incident. He guided us through a review at the scene of the tragedy and led us to evidence we could not have uncovered by ourselves. So I took the liberty of offering him a job at our Agency. I do hope that is ok with you?"

"Sure, that is fine with me. We can use all the steady and qualified people we can find. Well, you all go home and at least take the rest of today off from work. Nice to meet you

Jonas, you will like it here," Nora said.

"Thank you, ma'am," Jonas replied.

"Oh Blair, give me a minute of your time," Nora said as the men turned to leave.

"Sure, anything for you Nora," Blair replied.

"What are we going to tell the families of our men Albert and Nelson, in particular Alberts' family?" Nora asked him. "We had developed such a close relationship with Albert, it's like we are a part of his family."

"The thing that is most disturbing to me is that there were no bodies recovered. How can I face Jean with only a few of Alberts' personal possessions and a pile of bones that may not be his?" Blair replied.

"Let me know when you are going to see her," Nora said. "I would like to be there as I will be able to explain some things in more detail."

"That would be fine. I will let you know," Blair said.

"Ok. Take the rest of the day off and get some rest," said Nora.

The following day Jake, who had been away on assignment, returned to work and Nora quickly updated him on the case.

"Jean is going to take news about the tragedy at the ravine very hard. She loves Albert very much," Jake said.

"We will go together as a team to let her know what happened," Nora replied.

Blair had also returned to work and, in their team meeting that morning, Nora shared a summary of the information she had gleaned from the documents Lebron had provided.

"Lebron has documented a series of deeds, titles, and surveys, and tagged them as falsified. Other than Loop Development, he has not specifically confirmed anyone else responsible for the creation of these false documents. He indicated, however, that he suspects that the Police Chief and our Boss are involved with Loop Development. In the meantime he has logged the falsified deeds, by document number, on an Excel spreadsheet and cross-referenced each document number to each original deed. He noted that he is keeping the falsified documents safe as evidence," she told the team.

"Let's hope we can shed some real light on this Malutica situation soon," Blair said.

The team planned to visit Jean the next day in order to provide her with first-hand news about Albert. As such, Nora called her immediately after the team meeting.

Jean was glad to hear from Nora. She had been worried about Albert. She had found it odd that he had not called her but, knowing that there was secrecy surrounding the trip, she had concluded that he had been required to keep details of his whereabouts confidential as well as stay a little longer than planned. Now that Nora and the team would be coming to see her, Jean suspected that the news they were bringing would not be good.

Jean called Grant and asked him if he would be able to come by her house at around five o'clock the next day. Once she explained the reason to Grant, he also became uncomfortable about the situation and agreed to be there. Grant had been uneasy since he first found out that Albert had neither called Jean nor returned as expected. He knew that it was not like Albert to be so unpredictable unless it was way beyond his control. Now he was worried.

37

The following day Grant asked Wren to attend to his late afternoon and evening patients in order to keep his promise to Jean. He arrived at Jeans' house an hour before Nora, Jake, and Blair got there. Jean was just about to prepare something for the group to eat, but Grant presented her with deli sandwiches, cold cuts, and a couple bottles of wine.

Jean smiled.

"So thoughtful of you Grant. Thanks," she said.

"So, how are you holding up?" he asked her.

"The suspense is killing me, and I am now expecting the worst news ever. If the news is bad I know that I am going to be devastated, but I have prepared myself for the worst," she replied.

Grant and Jean sat on the couch and watched the evening news while waiting for Nora to arrive. When the doorbell rang Grant went to the door.

"Well hello Grant," Nora said on seeing him, "it has been a long time since I last saw you."

"Good to see you Nora," Grant responded.

"And here is Jake, and our man Blair," Nora said, as both men stepped into the house.

Jean stepped forward and they all hugged her.

"I know that you guys did not come to socialize, but we have sandwiches, cold cuts and wine. Let's partake before getting into the details of your visit," said Jean.

Grant, sensing that the team was hesitant, led the way to the dining table. He prepared a plate for himself, as well as a glass of wine.

"Come on guys, help yourselves," he urged.

Everyone got plates with sandwiches, except Blair, who only took a glass of wine.

"Jean," Nora began, "I deeply regret having to be the bearer of bad news, but I feel that having this news come from Blair, Jake and myself will be more comforting to you."

Nora paused and sipped some of her wine.

"When Albert was about ten miles from his destination, the vehicle he was in went over a cliff. It fell some fifty feet into a river infested with piranhas," Nora continued.

Jean gasped and put one hand over her mouth. Grant reached for her other hand and held it tightly.

"The authorities there did not recover the bodies, as only the bones were left. However, they recovered some personal items from the scene," said Nora.

Nora reached into the bag she had brought with her. She retrieved several items and showed them to Jean.

"Are you able to identify any of these as Alberts'?" she asked.

"Yes. The pendant is his, and also the bracelet. Adrean had given him the pendant a few years ago for Christmas, but where is the chain?" said Jean.

Jean was trembling. She broke into tears. Grant pulled her towards him so that she could lean on his shoulder.

"I'm sorry Jean. There was no evidence that a chain was recovered," Nora replied. "The items you identified will be given to you once the investigation is over, however. I assure you that you can depend on all of us from the Agency for all the support you need."

"Blair had gone to the scene and conducted an investigation on behalf of our Agency," Nora continued. "Most of the report he prepared is classified but, considering our close relationship, we decided to share it with you. This is because we always want to maintain the trust we already have between us."

Nora took a deep breath and then continued speaking.

"With the assistance of a young police officer in the precinct there, our Agency uncovered evidence to substantiate the fact that the incident was not an accident.

Instead it was a blatant act of murder. Bullet holes were found in recovered vehicle parts, and even in Nelsons' skull which was imbedded in the steering wheel," she said.

"Good Lord," Grant remarked, "that is so awful."

"He was so jovial and attentive that morning when he came for Albert," Jean muttered through tears. "I immediately decided that he was a very nice man."

"He was a very good person," said Nora. "Now I have the arduous task of locating his family and informing them of the tragedy."

Blair, who had been trying to hold back his emotions, spoke up.

"The police have been anxious to close the incident and classify it as being merely a car accident. I must say that their investigation was very sloppy. This incident must not be closed until the persons responsible for the murders are caught and punished. I, for one, will not stop until we get them all arrested."

Blairs' voice broke, and he roughly wiped away a tear that had begun to trickle down his cheek.

"I know you will," Jean said. "I know you will. I am lucky and grateful to have such faithful and devoted friends in you all. Albert had always made good choices regarding who he wanted to associate with."

"We will always honor our friendship with you, and you can be assured of our continued concern and support," Jake commented.

"Well, is there anything we can do before we leave?" Nora asked. "If you like, I could stay with you tonight."

"I will be fine," Jean replied. "Adrean will be home soon and Grant will be here with us. Thank you all for making it a little easier for me."

Grant saw the team to the door. Blair was the last to exit and Grant could sense that he was emotionally disturbed about the matter. He offered to see Blair professionally.

"Come see me anytime. No appointment necessary. Just call and let the receptionist know that you will be coming."

"I will," Blair replied. "Thanks a lot."

A short while later Adrean came home. After hearing of her fathers' death she burst into tears and went into a tantrum, and her reaction caused Jean to break out into deep long wails of pain and sorrow. Grant, known for his emotional strength, was now poised for a very long and tedious night. He immediately called Wren and explained the situation. He asked Wren to bring some medication to calm them both, as well as a change of clothes for him since he planned to spend the weekend there.

"We will be there as soon as possible," Wren said.

Wren and Dale hurriedly got dressed.

"Let's stop and get a few things at the supermarket," Dale suggested.

"That's a very good idea," Wren replied. "What would I do without you?"

"Just keep remembering that you will never do without me," Dale responded.

They hugged amid their laughter. They were grateful that they had each other.

When they arrived at Jeans' house much of the crying had subsided. Nonetheless Wren administered a mild sedative to both Jean and Adrean. Shortly afterwards they fell asleep.

"Dad, what really happened?" Wren asked.

"Come. Let's go into the den. We can talk there," Grant replied.

Grant, Wren and Dale settled in the comfortable den chairs.

"We were told that there was a car accident in which Albert and his driver had been killed. There were no human remains other than bones since the vehicle had fallen into a river infested with piranhas. A few personal items belonging to the men were recovered, however. The Agency Albert was working for suspects murder, and is conducting an all-out investigation," Grant said solemnly.

"Geesh. That is bad news. So sorry to hear," Wren said.

"We will inform family members and proceed to have Alberts' death announced tomorrow. This is a very unusual situation and requires us to provide Jean and Adrean with all the suggestions and support that we can. There is not much more that we can do tonight so let's try to get some sleep," said Grant.

Morning arrived with a more alert and active Jean. She was busy making breakfast long before the others awoke. Grant was impressed with the strength and control she showed under such tragic circumstances and hoped that she would be able to sustain it.

While enjoying breakfast, the group agreed to have a church service in honor of Albert. A funeral and burial would not be possible, since his physical body parts had not been recovered. They decided that if the investigation determined that any of the recovered bones were his, then the family would cremate them and preserve them in an urn.

38

With Albert presumed dead and out of the way, the Chief of Police, Follek, Flek, and Burns of Loop Development had expanded their operation. They had acquired many more properties in Malutica. There had been many rumors that Malutica was rich in gold and prime minerals, and these rumors had served to intensify their exploits.

A year had now passed since the tragedy and, with a significant amount of land in their possession, Loop Development was now poised to begin construction. They prepared applications and architectural plans to build a large shopping center and hundreds of middle-income homes in Malutica, with the intention of expanding on the number of plans in the near future. For now they intended to put all future deals to acquire land on hold until all prepared applications and plans had been submitted to, and approved by, the City of Malutica.

Lebron was responsible for reviewing applications for the construction of homes and businesses in Malutica, and he quickly determined that the plans and applications submitted by Loop Development were illegal. Over the course of eighteen months his team had obtained and safeguarded several fraudulent documents specific to property titles, deeds, and surveys, as well as the names of companies and persons involved in the falsification of those documents. Lebron immediately denied applications from Loop Development since they were specific to property for which documents had been falsified. Lebron informed Preston of his conclusions and called a committee meeting.

During the meeting Lebron contacted Nora and informed her of the latest developments.

"We confirmed that the Police Chief, Peter Follek and

Evin Flek are involved in the scheme with Loop Development. Loop Development has filed applications for permits to build on stolen land," he told her.

"Delay the permits for as long as possible but be very careful. These are vicious people you are dealing with. They will stop at nothing to achieve their goals. We are doing everything on our end to get the people involved with this scheme arrested but, since most of them are in high positions, we need to be absolutely sure that the evidence we have is concrete," Nora told him.

"I truly understand what it is going to take, and will keep you informed on developments here," Lebron replied.

As Lebron hung up the phone he felt a twinge of guilt. He regretted that he had not told Nora that Albert was still alive, but he did not want to risk doing so until Albert got his memory back. He somehow felt that Alberts' life was still in danger, and he knew that Albert was considered to be the most important person in the Agency investigation. He was committed to safeguarding his identify in order to protect his life.

39

During the following year Albert grew stronger and became active in many ways. Lebron had entrusted his care to the Chief of the community. Chief Choca was a man of great wisdom and integrity and was highly sought by many for his excellent decision-making abilities. It was the ideal situation for Albert to be in. In addition, Preston had assigned a nurse with a therapeutic background to personally help Albert regain his physical strength and abilities. She possessed the knowledge, skills and compassion that Albert needed to fully recover. Both she and Chief Choca provided Albert with constant and reliable companionship as he regained his strength.

The people of Malutica have maintained their traditions and way of life for many generations. Albert easily adjusted to their traditions and lifestyle. He and Chief Choca bonded in a manner that made them seem to be inseparable. They shared interests in nature, gardening, physical exercises, and the art of meditation.

The improvement in Alberts' mental and physical strength could be attributed to Chief Chocas' help, but the attention he received from his nurse Mara also played an important role. She had grown madly in love with him and he had developed a similar attraction for her. Their relationship developed and soon Mara was pregnant.

When Lebron and Preston heard that Mara was pregnant, they were confused. They had warned Mara about getting too close to Albert, given that he had amnesia, and had insisted that she maintain a strictly professional relationship with him. But Mara had felt that nothing could keep her from expressing her love to Albert and their love for each other had intensified when Albert, in turn, had expressed his feelings of love to her. He had no memory of his past and was ecstatic about the prospect of having a child.

Albert was energized. He now felt more connected to Malutica and was inspired by the new love that he had found. He embraced his gardening and exercise program with more interest and vigor.

One day, while on one of their riding trips, Albert and Choca were so engrossed in discussing expectations for Alberts' first child that they wandered many miles out of the reservation without realizing how far they had travelled.

"Let's go back," Choca suddenly said. "We have gone much farther than usual."

On their way back, they were approaching the area where the incident with the car Albert had been in had occurred. Suddenly Albert stopped. He had a blank look on his face.

"What's wrong?" Choca asked him.

"Something seems familiar about this place," Albert replied. "I have a feeling that I have been here before."

Albert shook his head in bewilderment.

"Let's head home," Choca suggested. "We've ridden for too long today."

The men rode home in silence. Albert kept thinking about where he had stopped and wondering why it seemed to be such a familiar place.

That night Albert was overcome by a series of nightmares. Mara heard him moaning and rambling and awoke to find him in a cold sweat. She administered rubbing alcohol and got him to lay on his side. He quietened down and then drifted off to sleep.

The following morning when Preston stopped by to check on Albert, Mara told him about his restlessness the night before.

"Heard you had a restless night last night," Preston said when he entered Alberts' room.

"More like a bad dream," said Albert. "Yesterday Choca

and I rode by this area outside of the reservation and ever since then the area has been on my mind as though I have been there before."

"Places that you have been, where you were born, or even places that you have dreamt about previously will appear and reappear to you in one form or the other," Preston remarked.

Preston reached into his bag and retrieved a bottle of pills. He opened it, took out two of them, and extended them to Albert.

"Here, take one of these after breakfast and the other at bedtime. Be sure to just relax today. I have to be at the clinic soon, but I will check on you tomorrow."

"Thank you for everything, and for being so caring," Albert replied.

"I'm a doctor, remember?"

Preston turned to leave.

"My fat lady how are you keeping?" he asked Mara.

"Fine as can be," she replied, as she walked with him to the door.

"See that he gets some rest," Preston told her.

"I sure will, and thanks a lot," Mara replied.

On his way to the clinic Preston stopped by Lebrons'office.

"I think Albert is beginning to identify some places he had experiences with. Although minor, it's a start. It is still going to take a long time and be a slow process, but he will come out of his amnesia eventually," he told Lebron. "I suggest that someone observes him more closely from now on. With respect to horseback riding, more than one person should accompany him. It is a good idea for him to visit the scene of the accident periodically."

40

During the years following Noras' visit about Alberts' tragedy Grant had provided Jean with much needed comfort, advice, and support. In addition Jean had been a source of consolation as Grant strived to overcome the loss of his wife. The couple had developed a close bond, fallen in love, and were now married for over a year.

After getting married Grant and Jean had relocated to Trombago and built a house on the hillside. It had a babbling brook at the back of it. The small brook ran alongside the adjacent hills and the fresh running water rippled as it journeyed across smooth grey pebbles. The house was built on a one acre plot of land and was beautifully landscaped with flowers and colorful shrubs. Many fruit trees were strategically planted to complement the neatly manicured grass.

Grant and Jean were enjoying a happy life on the island. The peace and tranquility of their surroundings enabled them to find strength and comfort in each other, and slowly memories of the tragic loss of their spouses began to fade. They had developed confidence in each other and their relationship was based on respect, admiration and a feeling of total security, rather than on passion. Nevertheless their home had so much sensuality about it that the intimate and passionate moments they shared was sometimes hard to control.

While enjoying breakfast one bright sunny Sunday morning, the telephone rang.

"Hello," Jean said.

"Hi Jean, this is Wren. How are you, and how are you enjoying your paradise?"

"Very well. I must say that your dad will not let me do

otherwise," Jean replied.

"That is him, as usual. Good old reliable," Wren said.

"Hold on for him Wren. Give my love to the others," Jean replied.

"Hello son," Grant said into the receiver.

"Hi dad. It's been a while since I called, so here I am checking in," Wren replied.

"How have you and the family been keeping?" Grant asked.

"Everyone is fine and doing well. I have actually been very busy over the past two months. I am away most of the time since I have to attend several conventions and medical association meetings. Dr. Hall has been doing a tremendous job filling in for me," Wren said. "By the way, one of those products that Mary had been doing medical research on has now been approved and licensed in the United States. It has just been released to the public here for use as an antibiotic. I tried to contact her by phone a few times, but I was told that she was out in the field and that it would be a while before she returns to her home."

"Well what can I say, I have prepared and encouraged you both to be the best that you can be so I am not the least bit surprised about your achievements. You have both made me proud in so many ways. It's been quite a while since I spoke with her, and I often wondered if she was still out there searching for her magic potion. Guess I will have to keep trying until I finally get in touch with her," Grant said.

"I will do the same dad, and I will let you know if and when I do. So bye for now. Love to you and Jean," Wren replied.

"Love to you and yours too my son, and I will talk with you again soon," Grant said.

"You seem a bit flushed," Jean remarked when Grant returned to the table.

Grants' emotions were showing plainly. He was very proud of his children.

"It is something regarding Mary? What is it about

Mary?" Jean inquired.

"The research that she was working on was a success. She obtained approval and a license from the United States government to market the product she researched as an antibiotic," Grant replied.

"Oh my! That is good news!" Jean exclaimed. She hugged and kissed him. "You should be so proud!"

"I am really happy for her, God knows I am. She has devoted so much to achieve such a goal," said Grant.

"Her grandparents will be moved by such news. Let us go and break it to them. I want to see their reaction when they hear the news," said Jean.

When Grant and Jean arrived at Greffs' house he was, as usual on a Sunday, sitting on the front porch watching people pass by and alternatively reading the Sunday newspaper.

"Hi dad," Grant said, hugging him. "What's in the news?"

"Mostly the same from yesterday, nothing really new," Greff replied.

Jean gave Greff a hug.

"Hi dad," she said.

"So what brings you two here on a Sunday morning?" Greff asked.

"We miss you both and just want to see how you're doing," Grant replied.

"Smart guy," Greff remarked, "you were both here yesterday. Something is up."

At that moment Myrna joined them on the porch.

"Hi mom," Grant said. He hugged and kissed her.

"Jean, is he behaving himself?" Myrna asked. "Come, sit beside me and tell me what he is up to so I can straighten him out."

Grant and Jean chuckled.

"Now where should I start," Grant said.

"Not at the end," Greff said.

"I got a call from Wren a short while ago. He informed me that the research Mary had been working on was successful, and that her product is now licensed and approved by the United States government for use as an antibiotic," said Grant.

"That's excellent news. So what does that mean for her?" Greff asked.

"Well, her name will be recorded in the World Science and Medicine Book and in the International Journal of Medicine, and the drug will be patented in her name," Grant replied.

Grants' eyes brimmed. He choked back his tears. Myrna held his face in both of her hands.

"You should never be surprised my son," she said to him. "It was destined. Greatness is in our genetic makeup. Let's embrace this accomplishment as another milestone and hold it dear."

"I think there is a bottle of wine inside. Let's celebrate her success," Greff commented.

Myrna went inside and soon returned with the wine and four glasses.

"Here's to Mary," Jean said. "Her journey to a country far from home has been worth it, and her time over the years has been well spent. As a result the world will now have a new medicine to take care of illnesses. Cheers!"

"Your grandfather, bless his soul, always told me to pay attention to the animals and watch what they eat; especially the bees and the birds," Greff revealed. "The things they eat can also be ingested by humans. Plants are also living things, and even those we do not eat have some value to us."

Greff looked off into space for a while.

"Your grandfather loved the outdoors and was always planting and nurturing various herbs, spices and vegetables. It is not surprising that someone in our family also possesses such traits," he said.

"It really was her sole choice and her decision to do medical research. That just confirms that we really do inherit qualities from our ancestors. It is truly amazing," Grant remarked.

"Well, revel in and cherish her great achievement and the way she made us proud," Greff responded.

"I just had to share this good news with you in person, without delay. I know how much it really means to you both," Grant replied. "Anyway, we must go. It looks like it is going to rain any minute now."

Grant was right about the rain. As soon as he got home there was a heavy downpour. Jean stood at the window marveling at the intensity of the rain and soon began wondering how Adrean was doing since she was so far away from family and friends. News about Mary had awakened her concerns about Adrean, even though she chatted with her regularly.

Jeans' thoughts were suddenly interrupted.

"Thinking about me?" Grant asked.

"Yes, and no," Jean replied. "My mind strayed a bit to Adrcan. This rain is truly amazing though. It makes me think about you and about spending the rest of the evening in bed making love."

"I was thinking the very same thing," Grant said. He gently held her hand, and she responded with a firm grip. They watched the rain together for a while.

That night Jean and Grant made love in a silent and gentle way that was nonetheless full of passion. During their lovemaking they found a lot of self-assurance and felt a deep sense of gratitude.

The next morning they awoke entwined in a peaceful and meaningful embrace. The sound of the rain beating on the rooftop and the howling of the wind through the trees were persistent.

"How will you make it to work in this weather?" Jean asked.

"Work is the last thing on my mind on a day like this,"

Grant replied.

Grant decided to stay home. He and Jean had breakfast on the porch where they watched the rain, the wind, and the swaying trees. The rain poured and poured for hours.

"This is the hardest and longest I have ever seen it rain," Jean remarked.

"We are now in the rainy season of the year, so expect more of this in the coming months," Grant explained. "This is good for the plants and it also helps to clean the air we breathe, not to discount the abundance of water it provides to serve our everyday needs. Sun and rain are some of the things nature provides to nourish us."

"You are perfectly correct with your evaluation," Jean said, "and you are such a romantic. But you didn't mention that rainfall tends to make one feel like making love, which of course is just the way I feel right now."

Jean disrobed and, with a giggle, she ran into the house.

"Catch me if you can," she said giggling, and ran towards the bedroom.

Grant quickly got up and chased after her, but she suddenly stopped and pulled him to her.

"I hope it never stops raining," she whispered in his ear.

They made love until they were both spent and fell asleep.

The rain finally stopped in the early evening hours, and Jean and Grant decided to have dinner at the Himda Resort. It had been expanded and many attractions were added. As such it had become a regular dining place for many. The Resort now had fifty guest rooms, the swimming pool was widened, and the area around the pool was extended to provide more space for lounging. A garden with cascading trees and beautiful flowers surrounded the pool area. Nestled between the trees were benches where couples would sit and enjoy romantic moments.

"Dinner here is always such a pleasure for me," Grant remarked as he and Jean took their seats in the restaurant.

"I can understand why your mom and dad find it so

romantic here. This restaurant is beginning to have a strong hold on me too," said Jean.

"The entire island would affect anyone in that way. It is a place of such extraordinary beauty," Grant said.

41

Manzi and Dori were late for their ride with Choca and Albert. Choca sensed that Albert was excited and becoming anxious.

"Let's wait a little while longer," Choca suggested. "They should be here soon."

Another thirty minutes passed before Manzi and Dori finally arrived.

"We are sorry to be late. We had a couple of errands to run before coming," Manzi explained.

"Well if you are all ready, let's go," Albert said eagerly.

Almost one hour into the ride Choca suggested that they head back home, noting that they had started out late.

"Let's go a little further," Albert insisted. "There is a place I want to take a look at."

Manzi rode closer to Dori.

"I think he senses something about the area where we found him. What are we going to do?" he asked Dori.

"Let us see what happens when we get there," Dori replied.

A plane was flying by as they neared the clearing associated with the tragedy. Albert looked up at the plane, and then into the thicket. He held his head for a few minutes before dismounting. Choca also dismounted and followed Albert as he began walking towards some trees.

"I know this place. Something happened here some time ago," Albert said to Choca.

Albert walked on a bit more. He had a perplexed expression on his face.

"There was a car, gunshots," he said.

Then Albert began to tremble. His expression had changed. He now had a look of fear on his face.

"Are you feeling ok?" Manzi asked. "You look scared."

"I'll be fine," Albert replied. "Let's go back home."

On the way home Dori and Choca rode side by side with Albert at a slow pace, while Manzi rode behind them. When he got home Manzi immediately told his father what had happened on the ride with Albert. As a result Lebron met with Preston, and they both went to see Albert. They took a bottle of wine with them, pretending that they were there on a social visit.

Mara greeted them warmly.

"Come on in. Albert is in the shower. He'll be out soon. Make yourselves at home."

She went to the bathroom door.

"Albert," she called to him. "Lebron and Preston are here."

"I'll be right there," Albert responded.

A few minutes later Albert joined them in the living room. He looked refreshed, but tired.

"To what do I owe this visit?" he asked.

"We figured we would socialize a little, have a chat and a couple of laughs," Lebron replied.

Mara entered with some glasses on a tray.

"They brought a bottle of wine and some nuts," she said to Albert and then turned to leave.

"It is my turn to take a shower. It is always good to have you guys stop by. We cherish and value the true friendship you bring us," she said.

"So, let's toast to friendship and the comfort and security we all find in it," said Lebron.

The men sipped some wine.

"We heard of the discomfort you experienced while on your ride earlier today and thought we would like to have you share your experience with us," Lebron said.

"There is an area outside of the reservation that triggers a memory of my having been there before," said Albert. "I also get visions of a car being shot at and falling over an embankment. It's like a dream sometimes, and sometimes it seems so real."

"Do you still have nightmares, feel scared, and have headaches?" Preston asked.

"I do experience headaches whenever I think too much about the visions I get or try to figure out what it all means," Albert replied. "But when I am otherwise preoccupied, or around people, I feel fine."

"On Sunday we will go to the area you mentioned and see if we can determine if it may be associated with your visions and dreams," said Lebron.

Just then Mara appeared.

"You guys have hardly touched the wine," she said. "Too busy talking away as usual."

"Actually, we were waiting for you," Albert replied.

"Well you all have a very long wait. I am due in two weeks and my baby is not allowed to start drinking," Mara retorted.

"That's my girl, make sure he keeps that in mind," Lebron said. "Well it is getting late. Time for us to go. See you on Sunday Albert."

"Thanks for dropping by guys. See you on Sunday," Albert replied.

"What's on Sunday?" Mara asked.

"Oh they are taking me for a car ride. I guess it is to reawaken my memory somehow," Albert responded.

"They are very good people. You can respect their judgment and rely on their sincerity," Mara said.

"That is so true," said Albert. "I am so lucky and blessed to have you and so many good and faithful people around me. It is like this wine, very good. I should remember the name of it."

Albert finished drinking the wine left in his glass, then he put away the bottle with the remaining wine and washed the wine glasses. Soon he and Mara relaxed on the couch and discussed the baby that they were expecting.

"You had said something to Preston about having a son. How do you know that you are having a son?" Mara asked.

"I just know that we are having a boy, and I am sure that

is what we are both praying for," Albert replied.

"A boy will be great, but I will be equally happy if it is a girl," said Mara.

"Whichever one we are blessed with will get all the love we have to give," said Albert.

They held hands for several moments, enjoying the companionship they shared. Then Albert kissed Mara gently and they retired for the night.

42

A lbert and Mara awoke to a bird alternating between loud chirps and whistles that were lower in tone. Mara groaned.

"Will he ever stop?" she asked.

"I guess he is just happy and looking for love," Albert said with a chuckle.

"Well he is at the wrong house. I've already given all my love to you, and there is none left for anyone else, so he is totally out of luck," Mara retorted. "Go talk to him and tell him that I already have a mate. Maybe he will get jealous."

Suddenly the chirping stopped.

"See, he has gone to seek out another girl," said Albert.

"Wrong," Mara replied. "He has sent his friend to try his luck."

The chirping had now been replaced by continuous whistling.

Albert got out of bed and walked over to the window. He observed Choca strolling leisurely through the garden, surveying the newly planted vegetables. He had dropped by earlier than normal to take his regular morning walk through the garden and was whistling contentedly. Then he began to tend to the corn.

"There is a very large bird out there and he is stealing all your corn," Albert remarked.

"What are you talking about?" Mara asked.

"Come see for yourself," Albert replied.

Mara joined him at the window.

"Oh, it's Choca. What is he doing here so early in the morning?" said Mara, with a chuckle. "He seems to be having so much fun in the garden."

"I hope you are making enough breakfast to share," said Albert.

"I didn't plan to, but I'll make sure that there is enough," said Mara.

"Well, let me go and get your bird in here," said Albert.

Choca was surprised to see Albert up so early.

"Having trouble sleeping?" he asked him.

"No, not at all. We were awakened by the loud chirps and whistles of a bird. We were listening to him for a while, and then you came along whistling," Albert replied.

"I see," said Choca. "The garden is doing really well. You should have a very good harvest."

"Thanks to your experience and care," said Albert. "Come on in. Breakfast is almost ready. Mara will be so glad to see you. For a while she thought that you were another bird."

Choca laughed. He was fond of Mara.

"How are you fat lady?" he asked on seeing her. "Still eating too much?"

He kissed her.

"Oh very funny old man, you are too wise for me," Mara replied with a chuckle. "Come on, let's all eat before breakfast gets cold. This is my special recipe, so nothing is going to waste."

"I love this dish," Albert remarked. "It is very good. You should make it more often."

"Sure, I don't mind. I enjoy doing things like this, especially for my two favorite people," said Mara.

"Lebron and Preston have arranged to take me for a car ride on Sunday. I guess it will be for a couple of hours. They figure that I need to see a little more of Malutica," said Albert.

"It is going to take more than a couple of hours to see even a little of this place, it's really a large expanse. I was born here, and there are places I still have not seen. Anyway the experience will be good for you. You will find the beauty and peace captivating," Choca said. He wiped his lips. "Well, let me go. Thanks for breakfast Mara. I enjoyed it immensely, and I will check in with you on Sunday – but not as a bird."

"Thanks for stopping by old man. We love you," said Mara.

"I love you both also. Albert make sure that you keep exercising, and enjoy your trip on Sunday," Choca said.

Both men walked outside where Choca stopped once more and looked admiringly at the garden.

"The garden is really doing great," he said. "Which reminds me, I have to go and tend to mine."

43

S unday arrived quickly, and everyone had high expectations. No one was more excited than Manzi, who had done everything in his power to be involved in the trip. He, Lebron and Preston arrived at Maras' house and found Albert ready and waiting for them. Albert was also excited about going on the trip.

Mara was sitting on the porch knitting when the men arrived.

"Hello Mara," Preston and Lebron greeted her.

"Hello Aunt Mara," Manzi said.

After greeting Preston and Lebron, Mara turned to Manzi.

"And how is my favorite nephew?" she asked him.

She loved that Manzi addressed her as aunt even though she wasn't his aunt, and she returned the love by calling him her nephew.

"I am good, thank you Aunt Mara" said Manzi.

"How are things at the clinic?" Mara asked Preston.

"Things are about the same, except that you are sadly missed. And how are you doing? Let me have a look at you before we go," Preston said.

Preston and Mara went into the house where he checked her vitals. He noted that all her vitals were good, that the heartbeat of the baby was normal, and that Mara could still move around with ease.

"Everything seems to be fine but be sure to take it easy and be prepared, although I am sure you already know that."

"I will be fine," Mara replied. "You guys be careful, and hurry back."

"We sure will," Preston said.

Manzi was the first to get into the car. He made himself comfortable in the front seat.

"No Manzi, you ride in the back seat," Lebron said to him. "Albert will be riding in the front seat."

As they were about to drive off Choca rode up.

"I see you guys are heading out on your trip," he said.

"You are welcome to join us," Lebron replied.

"Maybe next time. I will see you all when you get back," Choca replied.

"Ok. See you when we get back," Lebron said.

Lebron slowly drove away, with each of the men wondering what to expect or achieve from the outing. They drove in silence for a while, during which time Preston keenly observed Albert and tried to decide on a topic to broach with him.

"How are you feeling lately?" he finally asked him. "Any dreams or nightmares?"

"Not really," Albert replied. "Sometimes I get a vision of a helicopter and of guns, and also of a fireball around me, but it is vague and doesn't last very long. "

"So you are going to be a father soon. How are you feeling about that?" Preston asked.

"Nervous, I guess, about having a son," Albert replied.

"Are you sure it's going to be a boy?" Preston asked.

"I am sure it is going to be a boy. All signs point to a son. But whether it is a girl or a boy, I am really excited. Mara is a great person. I have grown to love her quite a lot, and I plan to marry her after our child is born. I know that you all will be happy for us," Albert said.

"We already consider you to be a part of our family, and I can honestly speak for everyone else when I say that you have been accepted as one of us," Preston said.

The car was now approaching a fruit stand on the side of the road. An assortment of fresh fruits and vegetables were attractively arranged on several tables.

"Let's stop and get a few goodies for the trip," Preston suggested.

"What time do you guys close shop?" Lebron asked the vendor.

"We will be here until evening," the vendor replied.

"Okay. Just a couple of fruits for now. We will stop for more to take home on our way back," Lebron said.

The men munched on fruits as they continued on the trip.

"It is so peaceful and beautiful here. I hope that it will remain this way forever," Albert commented.

"Look dad!" Manzi suddenly exclaimed. "Over there!"

"I see son. We will drive a little further and then turn back," Lebron replied.

Lebron drove for another four miles and then headed back to the area Manzi had pointed out. He was driving much slower now. As he drove Albert suddenly became tense and very quiet.

"I think I've been here before," he finally mumbled softly, looking toward the area where the vehicle in the incident had been shot at. "There was a car, a helicopter, gunshots. Let's get out and go for a walk."

The men got out of the vehicle and Preston pulled his camera from his bag. As they walked, he took several photographs. Suddenly Albert stopped and pointed.

"That thicket over there," he said with a look of fright on his face.

Manzi took Lebron aside.

"That is where we found him," he said.

Preston took photographs of the thicket as well as of the surrounding area.

"Let's go closer," said Lebron.

The men walked into the thicket. Albert felt tense and nervous, and Preston watched him closely.

"That tree over there!" Albert suddenly exclaimed.

The men walked over to the tree.

"Does this tree mean anything to you?" Lebron asked Albert.

Albert looked up into the tree and then held on to it as if to climb it.

"Go ahead, don't be scared," Lebron urged him. "Maybe

it means something if you do."

Albert climbed a short distance up the tree. He paused and then looked across the treetops. Then he descended. He was trembling, pale, and sweating.

"Let's go home," he said. "I'm having a headache."

"Here take these, they will help," Preston said, handing him a couple of pills. "Manzi, run to the car and get a bottle of water. Here are the keys, you can drive the car back here."

"Wait Manzi. Let's all walk back to the car together. I want to see things along the way that we probably wouldn't see if we are in the car," said Albert.

"Are you sure that you can do this?" Lebron asked him. Albert nodded.

"Yes, something tells me that I have to see the area at close range."

The men turned to walk back to the car. Suddenly Albert stopped.

"Here. The car I was in stopped here," he said, "and then it disappeared. The helicopter then took off. It all seemed so strange."

"Okay. That's enough for the day," Preston said. "Take the pills Albert, they will make you feel better."

Preston turned to Manzi.

"When we get back to the car you can sit in the front seat with your dad, and Albert will sit in the back with me. I know that you want very much to be in the front seat," he said to him.

On the way home the men stopped at the fruit stand and purchased fruits and vegetables for their families. As they pulled into Maras' driveway, Dori came running towards the car. She had an excited look on her face.

"What's the matter?" Manzi asked her.

"It's a boy! Mara had a boy!" Dori exclaimed. "Mommy and Chief Choca helped her to deliver a pretty baby boy, and he is crying for his daddy!"

Preston ran into the house to see if everything had gone well. He checked Mara and the baby and was satisfied that they were both fine, and that there were no complications resulting from the birth. Albert, who was still drained from his experience on the trip, walked slowly into the house. He kissed Mara and held her hand firmly.

"How are you doing?" he asked her.

"I am fine, and so is your son," said Mara. "Isn't he beautiful?"

"He sure is," Albert replied, and he tenderly touched the babys' hand. At that same moment they all heard the bird loudly chirping in the backyard.

"That bird is back again? Guess he wants to welcome our child into the world," said Mara.

Albert looked at Mara, then at his son. He had a blank expression on his face.

"I'll be right back," he said. "Preston, can I talk with you for a minute?"

"Sure," said Preston.

The two men left the room and went into the hallway.

"What's the matter?" Preston asked.

"Somehow I sense or feel that I have another child somewhere and that I had another life before now. Can you tell me what is going on with me? Some days I feel secure and at peace with myself, and on other days it's like I am transformed into a different person," said Albert.

"Do you remember when you were sick, and how sick you were? You are now getting to the stage where you are healing completely. For now, enjoy Mara and your son. On Sunday we will all get together and determine if there are any more changes in your condition," said Preston.

During the week that followed Albert was busy being attentive to, and caring for, Mara and his newborn son Martel. In the afternoons Manzi and Dori stopped by after school to stay with the baby before going home, and Albert would then spend time in the garden with Choca.

"This garden reminds me of a place I have been. Do you find me strange or crazy?" Albert said to Choca one afternoon.

"Oh no, no. The Creator has made many places and many people to look alike. There is only one sun and only one moon, however. There are no look-a-likes for those. The Creator will provide similar results for everything else, as long as you ask him to," Choca replied.

"You are a very wise man. How is it that you never ask for anything?" Albert responded.

"Oh, but I do ask. I always ask the Creator to give me the strength, the wisdom, and the good health to help others with whatever needs they might have. I do ask," said Choca. "You ask him too, and I am sure that he will bless you with the answers you need. He has already in some ways, without you asking, but ask him when you can and don't forget to thank him."

44

S unday arrived and many friends dropped by throughout the day bringing gifts, well wishes, and lots of love for Albert, Mara and Martel. In the afternoon Lebron and his wife dropped by with dinner. The table was set, and the friends sat down, heartily ate the scrumptious meal, and enjoyed the fruit drink prepared from the fresh fruits that had been purchased at the fruit stand.

One by one some of the friends began to leave, and thank you was echoed all around. Lebron had arranged for Alberts' closest friends to stay behind and, on cue from him, Preston spoke.

"First, let me again congratulate Albert and Mara on the birth of their son Martel. All of us wish this new family the very best."

"Yes, yes, we do," Lebron said.

Albert and Mara smiled.

"Thank you for all your kindness and support," Albert said.

"Albert has shared a number of concerns with me over the past few weeks. As a doctor I discussed these concerns with him on the basis of his injuries," Preston continued. "When Lebron called me about four years ago to attend to someone he had at his home I arrived there and found Albert bleeding internally and externally, and in a coma with broken ribs, a broken collar bone, and a big gash on his forehead. I immediately treated him for all the complications I found. He was transferred to Chocas' home for recovery and Mara was assigned as his nurse to facilitate his rehabilitation and support the therapy that Choca was to provide. Lebron asked us all not to tell anyone about this, as Alberts' life might be in grave danger. A day later Albert came out of his coma. We soon realized that he was suffering from amnesia, and I was unable to determine how long he would be affected by memory loss. Until recently Albert has had no recollection of what happened to him or who he was before his memory loss. Now he has begun to recognize a few of the places and past events that have appeared in his visions. I am totally dedicated to working with him, physically, mentally and psychologically, to ensure his complete recovery. I will now let Lebron take you through the delicate non-medical issues related to Alberts' situation."

"As Preston stated, this is a very delicate situation and I will try to keep handling it in the best possible way," Lebron began. "Remember that so called car accident that occurred several years ago a few miles outside of the reservation? Well, myself and several others came to the conclusion that it was not an accident after all. Albert had made an appointment to meet with us regarding the fact that our land was being stolen. Evidence shows that the vehicle he was travelling in was shot several times and then pushed over the embankment into the ravine below. Somehow Albert had escaped from the vehicle before it was shot at and Manzi and Dori found him lying on the ground under a tree. Based on his injuries we believe that he may have originally climbed into the tree and then fallen to the ground. Manzi and Dori had the good sense and judgment to bring him home to me since they did not know what to do about his injuries and his condition. I am sure that my decisions and actions might be debated, but I firmly believed then that his life was in grave danger, and I still believe that. As such, my only recourse has been to keep his whereabouts a secret until we find out who might want to harm him. Unfortunately at this time Albert is not able to provide us with any information to help us to determine this. As we all know, he has been suffering from amnesia. It may seem unfair for us to not have returned him to his home and family, but again, I firmly believe that his life would have been taken if we had done so. I am sure that his family has gone through quite a lot, since the police told them that he had died in the accident and provided them with a death certificate. I can just imagine how devastating it must have been for them to not even have received his body. This brings us to the problem that he and Mara now face. Albert has two lives – his past that he has no recollection of, and the one he presently embraces."

"So when will it be possible for me to know and face my past?" Albert asked.

"Preston will be able to determine that based on the improvements you make as you continue to recover. In the meantime I will be working to determine who I can put my trust in regarding your life," Lebron replied. "By the way, this is your wallet. It contains your badge and identification. See if you recognize the photographs in there."

Albert looked through the wallet.

"I have a feeling that I should, but I am not sure. Is this my family? My wife and child?" Albert asked.

"Yes, and let me explain about the badge," Lebron replied. "You were working for an Agency that protects the human and civil rights of people. You were working on a very important case that would expose some very important people. It is sad to say, but some of these important people are employed by the same Agency with which you are employed and they will stop at nothing to prevent anyone from making a case against them. Indications are that they found out that you were coming here to gather information and decided to stop you at all costs. They had to prevent you from reaching your destination. Keeping you alive was not an option."

"This is your briefcase," said Lebron. "Look through it often. See if the contents, as well as the photograph of your family, will trigger your memory. Let us know if and when you remember anything; let us know, and we will work with you."

"Not remembering is one factor. How will I deal with it

if and when I do remember?" Albert asked.

"You will not have to deal with it alone," Preston responded. "Everyone here is prepared to assist, guide and support you with any problems you may have."

"I know I have your support, but will I be capable of handling it?" said Albert.

"After listening to you all let me point out that we all must remember that we each have a destiny and a final destination. At the end of each road toward that destination we each must decide which way to go. If you ask for divine guidance, Albert, I am sure that you will be led in the right direction. When you reach the end of each road look at the signs and you will know where you are, and you will know what to do when you are there," Choca interjected.

"I thank you all for the support and patience that you have devoted to my well-being. I do hope that somehow, someday, and in some way, I can repay you all," Albert said.

"To know that we are able to help is extremely satisfying to us, and to have you back to your normal self is all the repayment you need to give to us," said Choca. "It has been quite a day. We have certainly covered a lot and it is time for us to let Albert and his family enjoy the rest of the day together. We will be doing this again soon."

"When is Albert going to get well?" Manzi asked his father on their way home.

"It is going to take time my son," Lebron replied.

"Will he stay here with us or go back to where he came from?" Manzi asked.

"At some point he may have to go back, but he is the one to decide about that," said Lebron.

"But he has Mara and his son," Manzi persisted.

"We made him aware of the situation and I am sure when the time comes he and Mara will do what is best for them," said Lebron.

"I hope he decides to stay here. I like him a lot." Manzi said. "The Agency you said he was working for; do they have authority over the Reservation?"

"Yes they do son, not only here, they have authority over the entire country," Lebron replied.

"I would like to do the things that Albert does to help people," said Manzi.

"You can someday. If you keep going to school, study very hard, and stay out of trouble, you can achieve all the things you want," Lebron said.

"I promise you I will dad. It is something that I really want to do," Manzi said.

45

During the months that Mary was in the field she had identified and labeled many plants and trees for research purposes. She and her team had steadfastly taken samples back to the laboratory and secured them for the time when they would end all fieldwork. That day had now finally arrived. Mary returned home with plans to revel in a long hot bath and some well-earned relaxation.

As soon as she arrived home, she heard her telephone ringing. She hurried inside and picked it up.

"Hello," she spoke into the receiver.

"Hello darling, this is your dad," Grant responded.

"Hi dad, how are you?" Mary asked.

"We are all fine. I've been trying to reach you for the longest while," said Grant.

"Oh, I've been out in the field. As a matter of fact, I just got home. Is anything wrong?" Mary said.

"Oh no," Grant replied. "Everything is fine. We got news of your success and have been trying to reach you to convey our warmest congratulations. But I guess it is never too late. The drug resulting from your experiments has been approved by the United States government and is now on the market here."

"That is great news to come home to!" Mary exclaimed. "It is even better to get the news from my own sweet dad. I knew that some other countries had approved it a while ago, but to have approval from the United States government is a great step forward."

"So when are we going to see you? It has been a very long time since we were together, and it would be great if we could all get together soon and celebrate your success," said Grant.

"It won't be too long now. I have a few months of

research ahead of me, but I will certainly make some time to be with you all soon," Mary replied.

"I am anxiously looking forward to seeing you. I love and miss you, so take good care of yourself. Here is Jean, she has been impatiently waiting to extend her congratulations," said Grant.

"Hi honey, how are you doing?" Jean asked Mary.

"I'm doing fine, only missing you all very much," Mary replied.

"Well we can take care of that very easily. Let us know of your next time off and we will have you here to laze about," said Jean.

"That is a deal I am not going to pass up. I really could use some relaxation and, more importantly, the chance to be with you all. I totally wish that I could be there at this very minute since I am exhausted from being out in the field for such a long time," Mary responded.

"Well get as much rest as possible and try not to overdo it. Congratulations on your success. Keep on making us proud. We look forward to seeing you at the earliest," Jean said.

46

M any months went by without any notable events in the lives of Albert and Mara until one fateful day when Albert and Choca were working in the garden and they heard an explosion in the surrounding hills. The noise startled both men and caused Albert to begin quivering, with a fearful expression on his face. Choca immediately grabbed him and supported him so that he could walk into the house. Suddenly there was a second explosion.

Mara acted quickly. She and Choca hoisted Albert into bed and she administered a warm compress to his forehead. Then she called Preston, who arrived a short while later. Mara and Choca explained what had happened.

Preston gave Albert an injection and began asking him a series of questions.

"Do you know who I am?"

"Yes, you are a doctor," Albert replied.

"And what is my name?"

"Preston," Albert replied.

"And do you know who these people are?"

"Sure. He is Choca, and she is Mara; holding my son," said Albert.

"Do you know who you are?"

"I am Albert Noble, and I remember having an accident that brought me here. I have to get home as soon as possible. My family must be worried sick about me," Albert replied.

"Let me get Lebron over here and we will work out some details with you. But for now stay in bed and do not overreact. Try to be as calm and relaxed as possible. We have to prevent the possibility of a stroke. If all goes smoothly, and with some care, you should be as well as can be," Preston said.

Later that afternoon Lebron arrived to meet with them.

"How are things going?" he asked Albert. "I understand that you are remembering things from your past more clearly now?"

"I can distinguish some memories quite clearly now, and I am now able to put a few of them into perspective," Albert replied.

"Let me ask you this," said Lebron. "Do you know why you were sent here, and who your driver was?"

"Yes I do. My mission was to have a meeting with you and your committee to get information regarding a case we were working on. My driver was Nelson, a trusted, loyal and likable person. I grieve to know that he died in that vehicle. I witnessed the events that led to his death," said Albert. "On our way here we were shot at by someone in a helicopter when we were just a few miles from the reservation. Nelson steered the vehicle off the road into a thicket and told me to jump from the vehicle the minute he slowed down. I did so and hid in a tree. His brave act is part of the reason I am here today. As the vehicle exited the thicket and entered a clearing, gunshots from the helicopter hit it from different angles. Then the helicopter landed after the vehicle came to a stop. Two men disembarked and fired more gunshots at the two men in the vehicle, who I presumed were already dead from the earlier barrage of gunshots they had fired when the helicopter was in the air. They then pushed the vehicle over the embankment, got back into the helicopter, and took off. After that I tried to get down from the tree. That's when I fell and blacked out. Oh, by the way, there was a guy by the name of Manny in the front of the vehicle with Nelson. I am sure he died."

Mara gasped.

"Are you sure about his name?" asked Lebron.

"Very sure," Albert replied. "He told me that he knew you, that he lived on the reservation, and that he had been out of town visiting his father."

"Oh no!" Mara exclaimed. "Not Manny!"

"Manny is Chocas' grandson and Maras' brother," Lebron explained. "We have been asking around for him for years now and have been worried, but we resigned ourselves to thinking that he had permanently moved away. He loves his father very much and had always been hankering to move closer to him, so that's what we thought he had done. He was a very good person. Choca is going to take this very hard."

Mara was sobbing quietly.

"Come, sit on the bed beside me," Albert said to her.

"Okay, here is the information we had gathered for your Agency. There is a development company called Loop. It is run by some very shady characters. They have influence in quite a number of government agencies, even the one to which you are employed. They have so much influence that they were able to get property lines rezoned, property titles and deeds changed, and people dislodged from their homes. My office has found new names appearing on titles for land that we know belong to specific people in Malutica. In addition we have original surveys of properties with the original boundary lines, as well as new surveys of the same properties with fictitious boundary lines. My office has also gathered evidence of mining operations that have been undertaken on thousands of acres of land that were stolen. I am not surprised that it was one of the explosions from the mining operations that triggered your memory. We now know for certain that Loop Development, some people from your Agency and from the police department, and possibly others that we have not yet identified are involved in this scheme," said Lebron.

"Now that we have all this information, I am sure that we can make some arrests and have those fraudulent transactions overturned," said Albert.

"We definitely gathered quite a bit more information since you arrived. But you have been away for so long, who can now execute an arrest program?" said Lebron.

"Remember your life is still in danger, although you are presumed dead. All your confidantes may now be unreliable. Who in your Agency can you trust the most?"

"There is Nora and Blair – I swear for those two – and there is also Jake," Albert replied.

"Ok. Here is what we will do. I will call Nora and tell her that I would like a private meeting with her and Blair. I will advise her to choose a private residence in the city for us to meet, as well as a day and time to meet. I won't mention anything about you, as we want this to be as safe as possible for you. Remember, there are people in your Agency involved in this scheme. Let me set it up and we will take it from there," said Lebron.

Albert and Mara stayed up for many hours that night discussing Alberts' breakthrough. The news that Manny had died in the accident was unnerving and they both decided to break the news to Choca in person, rather than do so by telephone right away. Furthermore they had to face Alberts' predicament head-on. He was torn between his past life and his present circumstances. He loved Mara and had told her that many times over the years, but he had a life before and he also knew how he felt about that prior life. Would his prior life be the same once he went back to it? What might face him then? Mara assured him that she would honor any decisions he made, and that her love for him would always be there even if he decided to permanently return to his prior life.

Albert was touched. He thought, I have really spent the past few years of my life with a remarkable woman. In fact all the friends I have made here have been truly remarkable. He decided to continue enjoying his present circumstances, including his gardening and his meditation sessions with Choca, until he was well enough to face his former life once more. Even so, he was anxious for that day to arrive.

The following morning, when Choca arrived to check on the garden, Mara broke the news about Mannys' death.

Tears swelled in Chocas' eyes. He said nothing at first, but quietly hummed a tribal tune for several minutes while focusing on a point in the distance. Then he took Maras' hand in one of his, and Alberts' hand in the other.

"The wisdom of our Creator is not to be questioned. It is steadfast and true. My grandson was a strong, kind and purposeful young man. We all believed that he was destined for great things. And he is; but not on this earthly plain. In death he has inspired us to be strong and persist in our lives, to overcome evil, and to prosper; rather than grieve over his death," Choca said.

Choca closed his eyes and inhaled deeply.

"To the heavens I commit your life my grandson. May your soul find peace, prosper with full strength and vigor, and achieve its' purpose in the heavenly plane," he said.

Choca began a tribal chant and led Albert and Mara into a deep meditation that soothed them all and brought them to a contented state of mind.

47

A couple of weeks later Albert, Lebron, and two Malutica community advisors set off for the meeting with Nora. Preston decided to stay behind since he was needed in the clinic. Lebron had briefed the community advisors – Keith Dryer and Aston Stone, who were former sergeants in the United States army.

Although the trip was long and tiresome, it was quite pleasant. The men enjoyed each other's company and took turns at the wheel to avoid an overnight stay. When they arrived in the city Albert was surprised at how much the area had developed in his absence. As such, they had difficulty locating the meeting place and had to ask for directions.

The meeting place was a large house situated on a half-acre lot. It was extremely private and well-maintained. There were two cars parked in the driveway when they arrived. As they parked and got out of the car, two men came out of the house to greet them.

"I am Blair, and this is Jake," Blair said.

"Well Blair it is good to see you again. Remember we had met in Malutica?" Lebron replied.

"Oh, yes, yes. You are Lebron. How lousy of me to not recognize you immediately," Blair answered.

"This is Keith, Aston, and he is Bert," Lebron explained.

Albert pretended not to recognize Blair and Jake. They were unable to recognize him because he now resembled an Indian. His hair was now long, he sported a moustache and beard, and he was much more muscular and tanned because of the exercises and outdoor activities he had been doing.

The men entered the house where they found Nora in the great hall. She was busy giving instructions to the household help.

"Welcome gentlemen," she finally said to them. "We

have secured this residence for your stay in the city. It is fully paid up for a month, but you are free to stay as long as you want to. It has everything you may need – five bedrooms, two bathrooms, a swimming pool, a sauna and a jacuzzi." She pointed to the corridor at the far end of the large hall. "There is a gathering room nestled in that corridor where we will meet in a little while. But for now let's go into the dining room where we have something for you to feast on. I guess you all must be hungry and thirsty after such a long trip."

As they walked to the dining room Nora pointed to an antique table situated in front of a bay window at the far right of the great hall. A fine china cabinet stood at the left of the table.

"We have a selection of wines and spirits for your enjoyment at the bottom of the china cabinet to the left of the table over there. I have also assigned someone to do the housework and cooking for you, so you should be quite comfortable here," she said.

The group proceeded to the dining room and enjoyed a scrumptious meal during which they exchanged pleasantries about the weather, sports and entertainment. Albert remained silent during this time but he noticed Jake glancing at him several times, with a curious expression on his face. However, Jake seemed to dismiss thoughts of asking him any questions.

After the meal the group poured drinks and went into the gathering room where Lebron shared the documents and photographs he had brought with him. Nora read each document and passed each one to Blair who in turn passed each document to Jake.

"This all confirms our suspicions that Peter Follek, the Police Chief and Evin Flek are involved in the scheme to defraud the people of Malutica. We suspected that Loop Development had been performing fraudulent acts for some time, and now we have the names of the specific persons associated with the acts. The photographs you provided are key. They will be critical when we have to prove our case," Nora said.

Nora glanced at Albert.

"Doesn't he talk?" she asked.

"He sure does, and he will play the most critical part in this investigation, more than the photographs will," Lebron replied. "I have something to tell you all that might leave me open to much criticism but at the time I decided to withhold this information I believed that it was the right thing to do. I still believe that I did the right thing."

After a pause and a sip of wine, Lebron continued speaking.

"Blair, remember when you came to Malutica regarding the accident? I had withheld some information from you. I was very doubtful about who to trust and decided to maintain secrecy about some things, so I couldn't tell anyone that Albert was alive. And Nora, that man does speak, and he is Albert. I will let him explain his ordeal," he said.

"Oh no," Jake interjected, and shook his head. "You want me to believe that?"

"It's true," said Lebron.

"It can't be. I would have recognized him long ago," said Blair. "You have to do better than that. Albert died in that accident. We got his death certificate and some of his possessions."

"It's true Blair," Albert said. "It's really me. In our meetings at the office we would write notes in our hands instead of putting them on paper. Nora and I would sometimes meet in our cars, and I would get letters from Bill Hall via Norm. We had to be careful because we suspected that Flek and the Boss were involved in a scheme. On the day of the tragedy there was a helicopter flying above us. It had the number six imprinted on it. Gunshots were fired at our vehicle from the helicopter. Nelson drove the vehicle into a thicket and told me to jump out, so I did. I climbed a tree to hide and to see what was happening. The people in the helicopter fired many shots at the vehicle from many angles. Then the vehicle swerved and came to a stop at an embankment. Immediately afterwards the helicopter landed and two men disembarked. They fired more shots at the vehicle and then pushed it over the embankment. The men then boarded the helicopter and flew away. Once the helicopter left and I was getting down from the tree I slipped, fell, and blacked out. I was told that when I was found I was in a coma and that when I finally came out of the coma I had lost my memory for several years until seven weeks ago. There was a young man at the gas station where we had stopped, and we agreed to give him a ride to Malutica. He was sitting in the front of the vehicle beside Nelson. I guess the investigators expected only two people to be in the vehicle and were satisfied when they accounted for two people from the wreckage. They figured that their investigation was therefore complete."

"My son and daughter were out riding that day and found Albert bleeding on the ground. He was unresponsive. They brought him home to us. We immediately called a doctor who determined that he was in a coma," Lebron elaborated. "The young man who died in the vehicle with Nelson was Chief Chocas' grandson Manny. Chief Choca has played a very big part in restoring Albert to good health."

Nora hugged Albert and broke into tears.

"I chose you for this mission, and it has destroyed your life. What can I do to mend it?" she asked.

Blair and Jake echoed Noras' sorrow.

"My God you must have gone through hell all those years," Blair said.

"You have our everlasting support," Jake added.

"Thank you. I know that you guys are here for me. But while my recovery has been long, with many difficult days, I actually found heaven," Albert replied. "Over the years I met and became closely connected to some of the most wonderful, loving and caring people there could ever be. I consider myself blessed and quite lucky. But I am deeply concerned. I have to know – what became of my wife and daughter? I must see them. There is so much to explain. For the most part they are the ones that must have gone through hell. Have you seen them recently?"

Nora looked at Blair.

"We were in constant contact with each other until a year ago, then somehow we lost contact. I am so sorry. But we will do everything possible to locate them for you. And I do mean everything. May I suggest that you keep your present appearance until we clear up this case? On Monday I am going to get arrest warrants for all the people involved in this scheme, starting with those at the Agency. I will inform you of the time and place where we will make the arrests, as I know that you all will want to be there," said Nora.

Nora, Jake and Blair soon departed.

"What great strength Albert has shown after all that he has been through. One would think that he would be defeated and be a broken man. I wonder, will he be back at the Agency after being away for so long?" Blair remarked.

"He sure can be, if he so desires. He was not fired, and he did not quit. His absence has been due to a job-related tragedy. But I doubt very much that he will want to return to the Agency. I do believe that he is destined for greater things. You can feel it in his aura, and he seems to be a much wiser person now; more confident and self-assured," Nora replied.

48

The showdown took place at the Agency on Wednesday morning. As promised, Nora had arranged for Albert and the three men in his group from Malutica to be present. With arrest warrants clearly visible in her hand, Nora walked into Folleks' office with Albert, his team, and Bill Hall.

Norm was in Folleks' office. Both he and Follek reacted with surprise. Nora explained the purpose of the visit and began to read Follek his rights. Follek interrupted, asking if he could retrieve his ID from his wallet.

"Sure, go ahead," Nora said.

Follek opened his desk drawer and pulled out a gun. Everyone froze, completely taken aback. Nora, for one, had assumed that Follek wanted to hand over his ID as an act of surrender.

Thinking that Nora was Folleks' target, Norm quickly lunged at him in an attempt to grab his hand and prevent him from firing the gun, but Follek raised the gun to his head and fired a single shot. Then he flopped. Blood oozed from the wound in his head. His lifeless eyes stared back at them and his right arm hung weightlessly over the arm of his chair. His gun had fallen to the floor and the sound of the gunshot reverberated around the room.

Flek was at his desk outside Folleks' office. When he heard the gunshot he realized what was happening. He quickly jumped up from his seat and began running to the exit stairway. He bolted down one flight of stairs and rushed out into the brilliant sunshine. Albert was right behind him. While in Folleks' office he had seen Flek through the side of his eye and sensed that he would attempt to run into hiding. He caught up with Flek, just as he was trying to open his car door.

"Where are you hurrying to? Have no time to stick around here? You will have a lot of time where you are really going," Albert said to him.

Flek responded with a right punch to Alberts' face and some kicks towards his groin. While the kicks missed Alberts' groin the punch sent him reeling backwards a couple of feet, but he was still standing. Albert recovered and retaliated with a series of right and then left punches to Fleks' face and neck. Flek had no time to recover from any set of the right and left punches. He also had no opportunity to return a counter punch. Albert was quick and thorough. Soon Flek recoiled and swayed back and forth before collapsing to the ground, battered.

"Now you will get all the time you deserve," Albert muttered.

Soon officers from several police precincts arrived. They rounded up three people from the Agency, as well as Flek, and escorted them out of the building.

News of the arrests were being aired on news media and, as a result, a large crowd had gathered in front of the building. They watched as the perpetrators were escorted to various police vehicles. Bill Hall had selected specific precincts to facilitate the arrests and had given strict instructions regarding the security that these precincts must ensure. He watched as the perpetrators got into the police vehicles and the vehicles drove off. Then he went back into the office building to discuss the next steps with Nora.

Things had pretty much quietened down inside the building, even though some staff huddled in corners whispering. As Bill was passing by Norm he noticed Albert drinking water at the water fountain.

"Who is that guy over there?" he asked Norm.

"I don't know but I can find out for you," Norm replied.

Norm walked over to Blair.

"Who is that guy?" he asked him.

"The one with the beard?" Blair asked.

"Yes," Norm answered.

"Well I think the case is at a stage where it is almost broken, so I can therefore take the liberty of telling you. But only trusted personnel must be aware of this at this time," said Blair.

Norm beckoned Bill over to them.

"Remember Albert who had been in charge of this case and was presumed dead in that Agency car accident years ago? Well, that's him. He is very much alive," Blair revealed.

Norm and Bill were both surprised and delighted to hear the news. They walked behind Albert as he walked to Noras' office.

Albert looked around Noras' office appreciatively.

"You've made a lot of changes. I like the new look," he said to her.

Albert then turned around and saw Norm, Bill and Blair standing just inside the office. He strolled over to them and hugged Norm.

"Hi Norm. It's me, Albert. How is your hearing?" he asked. "You made a very brave effort today. But Follek got the target he was aiming for." Albert smiled. "I see Bill is still at your side."

Norm nodded. "Good to see you sir," he replied.

Albert clasped Bills' upper arms firmly with both hands. "How are you Bill?" he asked him.

"I am fine. But am I seeing a ghost, or is it really you?" Bill asked.

"It is really me," Albert replied, and briefly related the tragedy that had befallen him.

"I suspect that your boss, the Chief of Police, was one of the men that fired gunshots at the vehicle Albert was in," Nora said to Bill.

"I could not positively identify him but, based on photographs I've seen of him, he could be one of them. As such, it is likely that the helicopter is from his precinct. It has the number six imprinted on it," Albert said.

"I would not put it past my Police Chief," Bill said. "He is as nasty as they come. We have enough on him to make an arrest, and murder would make it even nicer."

"Taking him into custody will not be easy because he is a very defiant person and has loyal men who might come to his defense. It could get really nasty when we try to arrest him. We had better not show up with only an arrest warrant," said Nora.

"Where did Norm go?" Bill asked, looking around.

"There he is, talking with Keith and Aston," said Nora, pointing to the three men.

"Oh those three," said Albert, "they are old army buddies. Norm was their senior sergeant and you will never find a closer knit set of guys."

"I do hope that Norm can come with us to arrest the Police Chief. He is one of the best men to have in such circumstances," said Bill.

"When do you plan to make the arrest?" Albert asked.

"Maybe on Friday. As Nora indicated, the arrest could be a nasty one so I think it best to have several of my men there. There are some dedicated men in my precinct that I would first like to make aware of what to expect and how to prepare for the arrest," Bill replied. "Do you guys have permits to bear arms?"

"It's short notice, but maybe I can get them. We have permits for Malutica, but we are not sure that they will be honored here," Lebron responded.

"Don't worry about the permits then. I'll handle that. The thing is, by now the Police Chief knows what took place here and what has happened to Follek so he is probably preparing for some kind of altercation. He is a selfish person with a nasty attitude. Where are you guys staying? Can I stay with you all until we arrest him? My life would not be worth a nickel if I should show up for work at the precinct today. I might as well take the rest of today, and also tomorrow, off from work," said Bill.

"It is still early in the afternoon," Jake interjected. "Why not let us go and arrest him now? We already have the warrants and, remember, he has access to helicopters. If he knows of the arrests here, and of Folleks' death, he might be getting ready to run. If we wait until Friday it might be too late. Perhaps you could somehow alert your men that we will be making the arrest today, and tell them to be prepared, to be very secretive about this, and above all to be alert."

49

A short while later the men arrived at the precinct. The officer at the front desk requested clearance. Bill stepped forward and presented his ID.

"You know who I am," he said to the desk officer.

Despite Bills' position as Chief of Detectives, the officer was reluctant to grant the entire group access to the building. While they were waiting for access Albert and Keith decided to go to the transportation area. Albert wanted to see if he could recognize the helicopter with the number six printed on it.

"Look," said Bill, "here are warrants for arrests we have to make. This is all the clearance we need."

Albert and Keith descended the short flight of stairs to the transportation area and looked around.

"That's it," said Albert, pointing to the helicopter with the number six on it.

They walked over to the helicopter.

"I remember the tragedy so clearly now. Nelson and Manny had no means of avoiding the gunshots that came from this helicopter," Albert said sadly.

Suddenly two men entered the area and began walking towards them. As they approached them Albert and Keith pretended to be working on the helicopter beside the number six helicopter. Then, before the men could board the number six helicopter Albert and Keith overpowered them, tied their hands, taped their mouths, dragged them to a parked van, and hoisted them into the van.

The Chief of Police was sitting at his desk in his office. There were three officers there with him. He immediately rose from his chair and faced Bill and his team when they entered.

"So what is it that you want that it takes an army to come and get?" he snarled.

"What we want we will get in court, but in the meantime we have a warrant for your arrest," Bill replied. Bill then read the Police Chief his rights.

"Officer will you handcuff the prisoner please?" Bill directed.

One of Bills' accompanying officers attempted to handcuff the Police Chief, but the Police Chief grabbed him in a chokehold and took his gun from its' holster.

Holding the captive officer tightly around the neck and jamming the gun firmly into his side, the Police Chief began walking backwards toward the office door.

"If you follow me, I will not hesitate to kill him," the Police Chief snarled.

He beckoned to the three officers who had been with him in the office.

"Come this way. The helicopter is waiting," he said to them.

The Police Chief scurried down the short hallway to the stairway, holding his captive officer tightly around the neck and keeping the gun jammed firmly into his side. His three supporting officers hurried behind him with guns drawn. The men descended the stairway and entered the transportation area through the back door.

"Shoot on sight," the Police Chief instructed as he hurried toward the number six helicopter.

Albert and Keith were sitting inside the number six helicopter, with the engine running. The two men they had overpowered had told them that the Police Chief had instructed them to have it ready for departure. They watched through the rear view mirrors as the Police Chief approached.

Suddenly the back door of the building opened and Norm and Jake ran out into the transportation area like a flash of lightning. They grazed the legs of two of the Police

Chiefs' henchmen to stop them from getting away. The men fell to the ground in agony, clutching their legs. They had relinquished their hold on their guns. The third policeman began running to catch up with the Police Chief who was almost at the helicopter door.

Once the Police Chief got to the helicopter door he immediately released his captive and shot him twice in the back. He then beckoned to Keith to open the helicopter door.

Keith opened the helicopter door and when the Police Chief attempted to get inside, he slammed his foot firmly under his chin. The Police Chief stumbled backwards and his gun flew up into the air as he fell to the ground. While he was falling he collided with the third policeman who had been covering his back and accidentally knocked the gun out of his hand. Keith quickly jumped from the helicopter, grabbed the policeman, and held him in a neck grip that almost tore his head off.

"ARRRGH!" the officer screamed.

Meanwhile Albert had jumped out of the helicopter just in time to see the Police Chief trying to escape. His gun had fortunately landed a safe distance away. Albert quickly caught up with him and delivered a vicious backhand to his head. The Police Chief spun around and responded by punching and kicking Albert. In turn, Albert delivered a series of counterpunches while deftly escaping subsequent blows that were sent his way.

The Police Chief was no match for Albert who wanted to punish him severely for what had happened to Nelson and Manny. Albert continued to administer powerful blows to his head long after he had stopped retaliating and fallen to the ground. At that point Bill, who had arrived with his team and had been watching the altercation, intervened. He placed his hand firmly on Alberts' shoulder.

"He is not worth anything now. He has just killed an officer. Along with the other charges he will face, he is looking at some very heavy sentences," Bill said.

Albert stopped administering punches. He rose to a standing position and walked a few feet away in disgust. He was out of breath but felt triumphant. He inhaled deeply and exhaled slowly.

"There are two men in that van over there," Albert finally said. "They were with the Police Chief at the time Nelson and Manny were killed. They are the ones who fired the shots that killed them. They are willing to testify in order to try and save their skins."

"Good," Bill replied, "that gives us all the men directly involved in the tragedy at the ravine."

Just then the officers from Bills' team were passing by with the Police Chief in handcuffs.

"Who the hell are you? I have never seen you around here before!" he snarled at Albert.

"I am your ghost – past and present – and not a very friendly one at that!" Albert retorted.

The Police Chief muttered something indistinguishable. He seemed tormented by the fact that he had failed to escape and had been overpowered by someone he knew nothing about.

"Who is that guy?" he mumbled repeatedly on his way into the booking room.

When the Police Chief entered the booking room he once more began asking who had overpowered him.

"We want to have whatever we tell you, and whatever you say, on tape," said the officer-in-charge.

Once the tape recorder was turned on, the procedure began.

"Have you ever been to a place called Malutica?" the officer-in-charge asked.

"Yes, many times," the Police Chief replied.

"Do you remember five years ago in Malutica when you and your men fired gunshots at a vehicle belonging to the Agency?"

"I can say yes, and I can say no, but what has that got to

do with anything?"

"Well one of the men sent by the Agency was not in the vehicle when you fired gunshots at it, and he witnessed everything that happened. He swore that he would work to bring you to justice. I guess he just did."

"Nobody is going to care much about some Indian reservation and bother to search for two dead bodies in a vehicle that is laying at the very bottom of a ravine filled with piranhas. Who would care?"

"He does, and we do, for we have recovered the vehicle with many bullet holes in it. And so my friend you are looking at two more murder charges."

While the Police Chief was being booked, reports of the arrests were airing on all news stations and Nora and her team were being hailed for conducting a thorough and effective investigation. The news stations reported that more arrests were forthcoming but that information on those was classified. Bill Hall was cited for heading a task force against his own police department and was questioned on the direction that the department would take as a result.

"At this time I have no answer to that question," he replied, "We have a lot more work to do and more arrests to make in this case."

Albert, Lebron and the rest of the team from Malutica listened intently as the news reports were being made.

"I think it is best for us to go now," Lebron finally said. "Let's leave the proper authorities to take care of the legal matters."

"We will stop by the house and see you guys later. There are a couple of things we have to talk about," Nora said, as Albert turned to leave.

"I need to take a long hot bath!" Albert exclaimed.

"You also need to have a haircut and shave," Aston replied.

"I think you are perfectly right. There are a couple of things I have to do, but certainly not while I look like this.

Let's stop by the nearest pharmacy and get a pair of scissors and a shaving set," Albert said.

"Don't forget, you will need some perfume also!" Aston added, as he maneuvered the car into the line of traffic on the main road.

The men laughed heartily. It had been an eventful day and they were glad to return to normality. The late afternoon traffic was slow, but it was a welcome change from the days' hustle and bustle.

Eventually they arrived at the shopping plaza. Albert made purchases at the pharmacy and then went into the department store next door where he purchased pants, some shirts and a pair of shoes.

50

The men arrived at the house to find it sparkling clean. Freshly made sandwiches were waiting on the table for them to enjoy.

"It is so nice to return here to such treatment after a day like today," Keith remarked.

"Don't forget, we earned every penny of it and more," Aston replied.

The men ate some sandwiches, drank several beers and then laid back on the couches in a relaxed mood.

"So who will do the honor of cutting my hair?" Albert asked.

"Don't let Aston cut your hair, he only does army cuts, and remember what happened to Sampson?" Lebron replied.

Keith chuckled and took up the scissors and the shaving set. He led Albert to a small room at the back of the house.

"Are you sure you know what to do?" Albert asked him.

"If you are not pleased when I am done don't bother to pay me, it is on the house. But I am sure that your date will be pleased to see you when I am finished," Keith replied.

"This is not really about vanity or appearance. I am the one who is not sure what to do. You have to realize Keith that I have been away from my family for over five years, presumed dead, and now I have shown up unannounced. What if my wife started a new life? What if my being presumed dead affected her emotionally? There are a lot of what ifs, and to complicate matters there is my life with Mara and our son. I am still searching for answers before meeting my wife again and, to a certain extent, I guess I will still have to look for answers afterwards," Albert explained.

Keith had always been highly regarded among his friends as being not only very smart, but somewhat of a realist.

"You should treat each situation for what it really is, and not with speculation. Taking a rational approach to every issue will always prove to be fruitful. There are changes for you to face and you feel a need to find a happy place, but with your strength, conviction, integrity and honesty you have already found your place. Here, lay back. Let me have a go at this beard," he responded.

"What you said makes sense," Albert replied.

"From your hair texture I can detect that you have a touch of African blood," Keith remarked.

"Well my father is from Scotland and my mother is from the island of Trombago where I was born. My mothers' father was English, and her mother was a native of the island," Albert replied.

"So that is where you got your toughness and your deep consideration for others," Keith said.

Just then Lebron walked into the room.

"You would be a very poor person if you did haircuts for a living, but I have to say it is looking damn good. I could use a haircut myself, but not today," he said to Keith.

"You are so right. This is my last customer today," Keith replied. "It's all done Albert. You can pay up front."

Keith gathered Alberts' hair clippings into a bag and handed it to him.

"You might want to keep this as a souvenir," said Keith.

The men walked into the living room.

"Good Lord! I didn't realize you were that handsome!" Aston exclaimed. "What the hell are you doing at the Agency? You should be in the movies wooing all those ladies."

Albert laughed.

"I'll be right back; into the shower for me. Keep those beers cold," he replied.

The men regrouped in the living room after showering and began playing cards. They recapped the events of the past couple of days and were grateful that none of them had sustained any injuries. Soon Nora and Blair arrived, along with Norm and Jonas.

When Nora saw Albert she gave him a very long hug while the others impatiently waited their turn to hug him. They were all in awe at his new appearance.

"Digger!" Norm exclaimed and hugged him. "It's really you!"

Albert laughed.

"On our way to Malutica Nelson had told me that some people in the Agency had been referring to me as Digger. I never knew anything about that or how it came about, and he shared his speculations about it. But I'm still not sure why I have been given that name."

"One morning I was in the Boss' office when Flek came in. They started talking and the Boss told Flek to keep an eye on you because you were digging into a case that involved them and that once you start digging you never seem to stop. Flek looked over at me then and the Boss said, 'Don't pay him no mind. He is just a deaf and dumb nigger.' I could not tell anyone about it because that would disclose the fact that my hearing was much better, but I will never forget it either," Norm explained.

Blair finally got a chance to embrace his deeply admired friend.

"It is so good to have you alive and well," he said to Albert. "By the way, this is Jonas. He was one of the young officers investigating the incident in Malutica. He is now working with the Agency."

"Glad to meet you Jonas," Albert said. "You are working among some of the finest people to ever serve our citizens and our country. Learn their methods and remember to always serve with dignity. So where is Jake?"

"Jake is working late with Bill Hall. There are a lot more arrest warrants – for Loop Development, Inset and several other developers and agencies – that need to be obtained, but they might show up here a little later. Come with me for a moment; bring your beer with you. Let's talk in the gathering room," Nora said.

Once in the gathering room Nora continued speaking.

"I have been trying to get some information for you, but it is coming to me in bits and pieces. So far I found out that Jean sold the house. I guess she didn't want to live there with the memories she had. You might know the person who bought it. She is Jeans' longtime schoolmate. Grant is now living in Trombago. He was offered a job as head of a hospital there, and he accepted. Wren is now running their medical office here in the United States. I have his number here for you. Maybe you should go and see him. I am pretty sure he can give you some solid information. I am willing to take you wherever you want to go whenever you want to meet with anyone," she said.

"Maybe in a day or so, but I can manage on my own to go back and forth. You already have your hands filled," Albert replied.

When they returned to the living room, they found that Bill and Jake had arrived.

"Now this is the Albert I know," said Jake, embracing his friend.

"I am very sorry about the things you went through," Bill said to Albert, "but I am equally happy to have you back."

"It is hard not to feel sad or sympathetic about my ordeal, but much good is going to come out of this," Albert responded. "The world is going to be a better place with honest and dedicated people like us in it to make sure that the civil rights of all people are protected."

The group chatted into the night, inspired by Alberts' belief that the rights of others will always be protected. They reviewed and clarified the next steps in the case. At just about midnight Bill and Norm decided to remain overnight in the house and Nora, Jake, Jonas and Blair departed.

51

Albert was once more driving past the house he had once lived in with Jean and Adrean. He had done so several times over the past three days and had not seen any activity. He slowed down as usual, but this time he decided to stop and make some inquiries.

A slender woman, around thirty-nine years old, came to the door. At first he didn't recognize her, and she also did not recognize him, but he shared information about himself and Jean with her and soon they both realized that they had known each other in the past since she was Jeans' best friend Ann.

"I bought this home from Jean two years ago. She and I corresponded for about a year after I purchased it, and then Jean told me that she was going away for a while. I have not heard from her since. I often hoped that she would give me a call, but she hasn't. Maybe she is somewhere in Europe since I think her daughter had gotten a job in the Ambassadors' office there. She never gave me details so I am not really sure which specific European country her daughter may be working in. Oh, excuse me, would you like a drink? Coffee, tea, or something cold?" Ann said.

"Maybe another time," Albert replied. "I have to be at a couple more places this afternoon and time is catching up on me. But thanks for the information. It is really good seeing you again after all these years."

Ann wrote her number on a piece of paper.

"Here is my number. Please call me if you happen to get in touch with Jean. I sure would like to hear from her."

"Ok I will, and thanks again," said Albert.

Albert drove away feeling despondent that he had not made any progress in locating Jean and Adrean at his old house. He also had no tangible lead to work with. He headed to the medical office now being operated by Wren, hoping that Wren could provide him with the information he needed. On the way there he wondered how Wren would react on seeing him, especially since he would be showing up unannounced.

The office building was much bigger than he remembered it to be and, to his surprise, it had been renovated to become a much more modern structure. There was a large counter in the reception area, with three receptionists stationed there. He walked up to one of them.

"Good afternoon, I am here to see Doctor Wren Ives," he said to her.

"Do you have an appointment?" the receptionist asked.

"No I don't. My visit is not of a professional nature, it is personal," Albert replied.

"He is away at a convention," the receptionist beside her, who had overhead the conversation, interjected.

"Oh, excuse my memory, Doctor Ives will be away for the next two months. You can leave your name and number with us, and when he gets back he will call you. Here is his card, you can also call in two months and find out if he is back," the receptionist said to Albert.

Albert took the card.

"Thanks a lot. I will call," he replied.

As Albert drove away he thought, I am hitting on nothing but dead ends, guess I will have to work things out when I get back to Malutica. He stopped at the shopping center and purchased gifts for Mara, his son, and his friends in Malutica. When he got back to the house, Nora was there.

"How did things go?" she asked.

"Not very good at all. I spoke with Jeans' friend for a while. She has no idea where Jean and Adrean are. Wren is away at a medical convention for the next two months. On the way here I decided that my next move should be to go to Trombago and try to sort things out," said Albert.

"You have my full support in whatever you decide to do," Nora said.

"I am fully aware of that, and it means a lot to hear it from you," Albert responded.

"Anyway I have something here for you," Nora said, and retrieved an envelope from her bag. "It is compensation for all the years that you have been ill, as well as salary for all those years. Now remember, you are still a part of the Agency. It is for you to decide what you want to do about working, and when. Take all the time you need to decide."

"Ok, thanks. I will be going back to Malutica the day after tomorrow and once there I will make arrangements to travel to Trombago," Albert said.

The next day the men went shopping and enjoyed touring the city before returning to relax at the house and play cards. They had a full day of travel ahead and planned to set out by nine o'clock the following morning.

Early the following day Jake and Norm stopped by the house to bid them farewell.

"I hope to join you guys in Malutica someday," said Norm.

"That's a good idea," said Aston.

"You are very welcome to come. You would love it there," said Keith.

52

Mara was busy washing clothes when Albert arrived home. She immediately stopped and ran into his arms. Albert reached out to his son, but he clung firmly to Mara and wouldn't let go.

"See, it's only daddy!" Mara said. "Isn't he handsome without all that hair and beard?"

Albert presented the gifts he had bought. While he and Mara talked, his son sat at their feet playing with his new toys and occasionally extending them for Albert to play with.

"It's amazing what a toy will do. I've won him over!" Albert said with a laugh.

"He seems to like his new toys a lot," Mara remarked.

"There is so much to tell you about the trip," Albert said. "What I have to share is going to keep us up all night."

"We will talk about your trip tomorrow," said Mara. "Right now all I want is to have you in bed."

Alberts' absence certainly had an impact on their lovemaking. That night he and Mara made love as though it was their very first encounter. Immediately afterward they fell asleep in each other's arms and slept uninterrupted all night until early the following morning when the loud chirps of the bird woke them up.

"Has he been doing this again?" Albert asked.

"No, not recently," Mara replied.

"How did he know that I was back?" Albert responded.

"He knows alright. He knows everything," said Mara.

At breakfast Albert produced the envelope containing the compensation and salary that the Agency had granted him.

"I want to put some of the money in the bank for my childrens' future, and also find a sound investment for some of it," said Albert. "It is so important for me to find my wife and my daughter."

Just then there was a knock at the door. It was Choca.

"Choca my friend! Come in, come in! So good to see you!" said Albert.

"Hi Bert," Choca said, and hugged him. "Glad to have you back and looking so good."

He turned to Mara.

"Hi Mara. I see you have found a new man! A good looking one too!" he said to her.

Mara laughed.

"Carry on old man. One of these days…," she replied.

Both men went outside. As they entered the garden, the bird flew into a nearby tree and began chirping loudly.

"See, he knows you are back," said Choca. "He is trying to tell you how much he missed you, and to welcome you back."

"I wish he was wise enough to help me through my current state of uncertainty about the future," said Albert.

"Maybe through him there is a message. Have you ever tried to listen to what he is saying?" said Choca. "In the same way that the bird is trying to make contact with you, you need to make contact with people. Everyone has a message."

"Thank you Choca. You and that wonderful bird may actually be my messengers."

Suddenly a memory of Grant had come into Alberts' mind.

53

J ean had, as usual, prepared a delicious dinner. She and Grant had decided to dine at home this Friday night, and enjoy dinner at the Himda Resort on Saturday instead. It was a warm and sultry evening and, although it was not yet dark, crickets were already chirping. The odor of the rain-soaked soil wafted into the living room where they laid on the couch relaxing after dinner.

"Care for some wine?" Jean asked.

"Sure," Grant replied. "What are you toasting to?"

"Us, I guess, and how we have grown on each other over the years. Life here, with the peace and beauty of the island, is like a form of therapy. The peace shows in the beauty of the plants, in the residents on the island, and in everything around us. Life here could almost be described as paradise. I am very glad that we decided to relocate here," said Jean. She poured two glasses of wine.

"Do you ever think of your friend?" she asked.

"Sure I do. Why do you ask?" said Grant.

"Do you miss him?" Jean asked.

"Every day I can think of," Grant replied. "It is hard not to think of someone you care for."

"Do you think he would approve of us being together?" asked Jean.

"I am sure he would. He would want nothing more than for us to be together, and nothing less would do," said Grant. "Remember when I lost Amy? For months he carried a burden and a deep sense of loss for me. Remember, we always cared for each other like brothers do. I am pretty sure that he would want me to look after his family and his families' welfare as if his family were my own. I don't think he would want it any other way."

Grant was perplexed by Jeans' expression.

"What is the matter?" he asked her.

"Nothing exactly really," Jean replied. "I guess it's just that you are both different, and yet you both seem to be the same person. I can't help feeling that I am so very lucky."

"You are with the person who loves you and that is all that matters. It is so good that we can talk about these things, as it makes us accept the facts as they are as well as what has really made us who we are. We must be happy with ourselves and the people and things we have around us," said Grant.

54

A lbert had been playing with Martel all morning. He had just shown Martel how to put his toys away neatly and was on his way out to the garden when the telephone rang.

"Hi Albert," Nora said when he answered. "I have to let you know about the changes that are taking place in the city. Bill Hall has been promoted to Chief of Police and most of his trusted officers were also promoted. The city now has new-found confidence in the police department and in the people running it. This all leads to a very delicate matter. I have been asked to head the Agency, but I think that you would be a very good candidate and that you deserve the position."

"Go ahead and take the job Nora," Albert replied. "No one is more qualified than you are. You have the experience, the respect, the attention, and the full support of everyone in the Agency. There is nothing for you to think about."

"It's just that I really want to have you back here given the circumstances, and in any capacity," said Nora.

"I am pretty sure that you are sincere but, without a doubt, you are the right person for that job. So go ahead and take it. Remember, I have a lot to straighten out in my personal life and it will take me quite some time to do that," said Albert.

While discussing the new position with Nora, and persuading her to take it, Albert realized just how close they had become and the value she placed on their friendship.

"So what are your plans?" she asked. "Have you made any progress regarding Jean and Adrean?"

"I have been running into a lot of dead ends," Albert replied. "But I will be going to Trombago in a couple of weeks. Maybe someone there might know something. As a matter of fact, I will be calling there in a little while since no one there is aware that I am alive. It is not fair that my mom and dad have been kept in the dark for so long."

"Well good luck with your new position," Albert continued. "I guess Blair and Jake will also be promoted?"

"Yes, Blair will be my assistant and Jake will take a step up," Nora responded. "Please let me know when you are leaving for the island, and if there is anything I can do to make things easier for you please don't hesitate to let me know."

"I sure will," Albert replied. "And thanks again for your friendship."

Albert hung up from the call with Nora and immediately called Trombago.

"Hi mom," he spoke into the receiver. "This is going to be a shock to you, and very hard for you to believe, but this is Albert."

"Who is this?" his mother asked doubtfully.

"Albert, your son," Albert replied.

"Hold on a moment," his mother said.

Albert heard his father in the background.

"Who is it dear?" his father asked.

"Some man pretending to be Albert. Here, you talk to him," his mother said.

"Hello?" his father spoke into the receiver.

"Hi dad. This is Albert," Albert replied.

"Albert? Albert who?" his father asked.

"Your son dad," Albert replied gently.

"My son? My son has been dead for almost six years now!" his father exclaimed.

"Yes dad, that's what the reports have said, but it's really me," Albert said patiently. "I can explain everything. I know it is going to be a shock to everyone but, as unbelievable as it may sound, I am very much alive. The circumstances surrounding my disappearance can't be explained over the phone so I will be coming to the island on the twentieth, which of course is my birthday. The things I have to tell you are shocking and quite gruesome. They are going to sound almost unbelievable. I wanted to contact you before now but was cautioned about doing so and advised to wait for a specific time. I am in good health and my life is no longer in danger. I just miss you both a great deal."

Albert paused. His father was silent. He could just imagine how he was feeling. He decided it was best not to continue the phone call for much longer.

"My search for Jean and Adrean has been futile. No one seems to know where they are," Albert continued. "A friend of hers thinks that she might be in Europe somewhere, as she remembers hearing that Adrean was working for the Ambassador to that continent, but she isn't sure what specific country she might be assigned to. Anyway tell mom not to worry. I'm fine and am looking forward to some Johnny cakes, fried fritters and hominy when I get there. Love you both and see you both soon."

"Hey, wait," his father spoke into the receiver.

But Albert had hung up the phone.

"Hell, he hung up the phone," Olan muttered. "I wanted to tell him that Jean is here on the island. Well maybe it is best that I didn't get to tell him that."

"Are you sure that was Albert?" Alicia asked.

"I would guess so. Who would know that the twentieth of this month is his birthday, and that you always make him Johnny cakes, fried fritters and hominy? He also mentioned trying to locate Jean and Adrean. Actually, we should go and see Jean and somehow break the news to her," Olan replied. "Get dressed while I call her and arrange to visit with her and Grant. I will also get in touch with Greff so that he can be there too."

"Hello dad. Grant's in the shower," Jean spoke into the receiver.

"That's okay. How would you like some company?" Olan asked.

"I would like that very much. This is a nice day to chit chat and socialize. I will let Grant know that you are coming over," said Jean.

"Oh, by the way I'm going to ask Greff and Myrna to come along. I'm sure they would like to join us," Olan said.

"That's fine," said Jean. "See you all soon."

Greff readily agreed to socialize with Grant and Jean.

"Great," said Olan. "I'll pick you up in an hour."

Grant, who was a bit suspicious about the visit, was standing in the driveway when Albert's parents arrived with Greff and Myrna.

"I have a feeling you people are not here to socialize, but to get us involved in some deal or other," he quipped.

"Far from that!" Olan replied. "We have some very important news that we just received and we must share it with you and Jean. Let's go inside. You both have to be seated for this."

When they got inside Jean greeted them with her usual hugs and kisses and offered each of them a glass of wine. Olan took a sip of wine and smiled with pleasure.

"Have you guys ever thought of going into the wine and liquor business? You have excellent taste in wines," he remarked.

"Just as I thought," Grant replied. "You want to get us involved in the liquor business."

Olan looked over at Alicia. He had a quizzical expression on his face. She immediately realized that he did not know where to begin. She therefore took the lead.

"Earlier today," she began, "I got a call from a gentleman claiming to be Albert."

Alicia paused as a palpable silence had descended over the room. Everyone, excluding Olan and Alicia, had expressions of disbelief.

"At first I thought that it was some crazy crank call, and was about to hang up, but Olan was behind me and was concerned so I told him what the man had said to me and handed him the phone."

"I took the phone from Alicia and expressed my

disbelief that the man was Albert," Olan chimed in. "I told him that my son had died almost six years ago. But the man persisted. He stated that he was Albert and that he was never dead. He said that he couldn't explain what had happened to him over the phone but mentioned things that only Albert could have known. He also said that he will be coming here in a couple of weeks, and that when he got here he would explain what had happened to him. Apparently he had been trying to locate Jean and Adrean and heard that Adrean was working with the ambassador to Europe so Jean was probably there too, but no one knew the specific country that Adrean was working in. I was about to tell him that Jean is here in Trombago but then he said that he would see me soon and hung up before I got the chance to do so."

Jean had a stunned look on her face and Grant was holding her hand tightly.

"Now that I have had a chance to think about this, it is actually a stroke of luck for everyone that I did not get to tell him that Jean is here," said Olan.

Jean covered Grants' hand with her other hand. They looked at each other questioningly, and their eyes delivered no silent answers.

"There is a logical reason that things happen, as well as a logical reason that things are destined," said Myrna. "We will always have difficulties and obstacles to overcome but with patience, and with understanding about how and why things happen, we can achieve peace of mind."

Myrna sensed the emotions that Jean and Grant were feeling and was sympathetic.

"There was never anything deliberate about this whole situation, nor did your marriage happen by design," Myrna continued. "Your situation requires a rational approach and I am sure that you will handle it rationally. Compromises and sacrifices have already been made, and more will be made. There is no guilty party involved here. At the end of it all no one will be left feeling guilty."

"Grant and Jean, I urge you not to let this news drive a

rift between you. That might cause a gap that can never be narrowed," Greff added. "As a result of this news you may experience tense, nervous and stressful periods. I know Grant is aware of that, since he is a doctor. However, I am sure that you will both be able to contain those times if they occur."

Grant nodded. He and Jean had been listening intently.

"We are not in a hurry to go, but I guess you would like some time by yourselves to discuss the entire situation and maybe make some phone calls and some decisions right away. Many decisions will ultimately have to be made. Remember, we are always here to help in any way possible," said Greff.

"I know that," said Grant, "and thanks a lot. I am pretty sure that things will work out positively, but I have to say that this is one hell of a surprise – so very unexpected. I know that I can handle the matter at hand, but Jean has already been through so much. She is strong enough to face it all, but she is going to need a lot of support and attention."

"You can depend on us to do everything we can to help," said Greff.

Grant walked the visitors outside and watched as they drove away. Meanwhile Jean had put away the wine bottle and was washing the wine glasses.

"Can you imagine this!" she exclaimed when Grant came back inside. "Why are all these things happening to me? Do I really deserve this?"

"No you don't. No one does. But let's not draw any conclusions yet. Despite all that was said we are still not sure how true the information is. Furthermore we have time to discuss the matter and prepare ourselves for the decisions that we may have to make. One way or the other I'm sure things will work out just right. Let us sleep on it tonight and tomorrow night," said Grant.

"We have to make sure that we call Adrean in the morning to break the news to her. I was thinking of calling her now, but tomorrow morning is just as good," said Jean.

The couple went to bed very late that night. In spite of this, Jean had difficulty falling asleep. When she finally did, she slept in short spells and tossed and turned throughout the night.

The following morning Jean awoke early, and with a sense of urgency. She was anxious to call Adrean, explain the situation to her, and then take some time to be by herself and try to figure things out.

Adrean answered the phone on the first ring. She was alarmed to be getting a call from her mother so early in the morning. She thought someone had died or something terrible had happened. When she heard that her dad was alive she felt more at ease, but she was bewildered.

"I will try to book the earliest flight possible and will call you this evening to let you know when I will arrive in Trombago," she said.

Jean spent the rest of the morning in the garden, where she could find peace with her thoughts and be confident in her deliberations. In the afternoon she sat with Grant and they discussed the situation and weighed their options. While they were talking, the telephone rang.

"Hello?" Jean spoke into the receiver.

"Hi mommy," Adrean replied. "How are you holding up?"

"I'm doing as well as can be," Jean replied.

"I requested three weeks off from work and will know tomorrow if my request is approved. In the meantime I've made reservations for next week Wednesday on Flight #376," said Adrean.

"We will understand if you have a problem getting the time off or difficulty making the trip for any reason," said Jean.

"Mommy, remember, he is my father and you are my mother. I have to be involved in anything pertaining to our family. I will be there at all costs, so keep strong and give my love to Grant," said Adrean.

55

Albert was thinking of taking his son with him to Trombago, but after discussions with Mara he decided that it was not such a good idea after all. However, Albert wanted a travel companion – someone to inspire him on the trip; he was just not sure who to choose. He called Nora, and rather than outrightly ask her to be his travel companion, he spoke speculatively.

"Have you ever been to Trombago? I am going there next week to visit my mom and dad and get my thoughts together under more serene surroundings."

"No, I have never been there," said Nora.

"It would be nice for you to experience the beauty of the island," said Albert.

"How long are you planning to stay there?" Nora asked.

"Close to two months," Albert replied.

"I won't be able to travel with you next week, but I can certainly get there two or three weeks later," Nora responded.

She would not say it, but she wanted to give Albert as much time as possible to be with his family before she arrived.

"I have always wanted to see what the island is like, so now is as good a time as any. I will definitely be there while you are there," she elaborated.

While enjoying breakfast the following morning Mara and Albert were discussing the trip that Albert would make to Trombago.

"I was thinking that Manzi would be a good companion for you on the trip. He is always hanging around you as if he is your guardian angel. That boy has grown to love and admire you very much. Perhaps you can get permission from his parents," Mara said.

Suddenly there was a knock at the door.

"I bet that is Choca. I know his time and knock anywhere," Albert remarked.

Albert opened the door.

"Come in," he said to Choca. "Come join us, we are in the middle of breakfast."

"Hi sweet girl," Choca said to Mara. "Did you make my favorite meal today?"

"Sure old man, I will get some for you," Mara replied.

"Grandpa have some of mine and you will get strong!" said Martel.

Choca smiled.

"Oh that looks so good," he said to Martel.

Choca pretended to eat from the spoon Martel extended. Then he pretended to chew the imaginary food.

"Yum, yum. Look how strong I am already!" Choca exclaimed.

Martel beamed with satisfaction.

"Before you arrived we were talking about taking Manzi along with me on my trip. What do you think?" said Albert.

"That's a very good idea. That boy adores you and, don't forget, he actually saved your life. In some ways he feels a strong bond with you. Haven't you noticed how much he looks up to you? I think he wants to adopt some of your qualities. A trip to the country of your birth will allow him to know more about you, and he will benefit greatly from being exposed to Caribbean customs and culture. He won't be able to get that experience here. You know, maybe Manzi could also confirm your ordeal since he has first-hand knowledge of it. You should go and see him this evening and get his parents' permission. I am pretty sure they will allow him to go," said Choca. "Let's go and see how the garden is doing as soon as we finish eating. I had sowed some pepper seeds, and I hope to start transplanting them soon."

The sun was bright outside. The men donned their shades and strolled amongst the vegetables.

"I can see that the pepper suckers are just about ready. Let's get them properly spaced. Then they should be fully established before you go on your trip," said Choca.

"I am sure that I can depend on you to take care of things here for me while I am gone," said Albert.

"Don't you worry. Everything here will be just fine," said Choca.

Soon the men finished gardening and decided to enjoy a cool drink on the porch. While Choca relaxed in what had now become his favorite chair, Albert went inside and returned with a jug of lemonade and two glasses.

"What if the conditions and circumstances you find in Trombago cause you not to return? Have you given that some thought?" asked Choca.

"They won't," Albert replied. "Although I have thought fondly about the island, there is nothing there that would diminish the love, affection, and satisfaction that I have found in being here with everyone. I affirm that the only place that I have found love, kindness, acceptance and the need to want and be wanted, apart from where I was born, is right here. Although I am going to the land of my birth, I am going there primarily to prove that I am still alive, to explain what happened to me over the past six years, and to enjoy being with my parents once more. My family in Trombago deserves an understanding of my misfortune and my grief as well as my hope for a brighter life. There is no greater love than family, and fortunately for me I now have a surplus. So you see Choca, I have to return. Remember your favorite saying – 'There is a place to find'? – well I truly believe that I have found my place."

"Do you realize that you have changed quite a lot over the years? Whether adaptation is a contributing factor or what I am seeing in you has always been there and is now coming to the surface, you have embraced and adopted a spiritual view of things and way of life," said Choca.

"Sure, I am aware of that. I have always had compassion for others as well as a will to help the less fortunate and the defenseless. I had sworn when I was a teenager that I would be helpful in this way. Given the right opportunity I will do so on a large scale, but I would use a different approach than that being used by government, organizations and so many people today," said Albert.

"For years my people have been searching for a better way to prosper in our lives, but we have always been exploited and prevented from advancing in life. But, with the dedication of people like Lebron and Preston, we now seem to be making strides in some areas. Malutica can be very valuable to the rest of the country. It has many resources, one of which is its' people. We are hungry for a chance to improve ourselves – our economics, our living and educational standards, our infrastructure – to name only a few. Until the government recognizes the needs of our people and honors the promises it made to us, we will always mistrust the system and continue to feel deserted."

Choca nodded solemnly, took a sip of lemonade, and then continued speaking.

"I am more concerned about the younger ones. They need to be properly educated, given a sense of direction and have more opportunities available to them because, if we lose them, we will also lose our happiness. On that note, I had better take off now. I will see you tomorrow," he said.

Choca rose and stuck his head inside the house door.

"See you tomorrow sweet lady!" he shouted to Mara.

"Bye old man, and our love goes with you!" Mara replied.

It was almost six o'clock and Albert wanted Mara and Martel to come with him to Lebrons' house.

"Martel is sleeping so peacefully," Mara pointed out. "It is best not to wake him for the trip. You had better go alone, and of course that will force you to come back quicker."

"Just for being so smart, I am going to take my sweet

time getting back," Albert said.

He gave her a kiss and she smiled lovingly at him.

"Ok my love. I'll be back soon," he said softly, and pinched her cheek.

Lebron was just pulling into his driveway when Albert drove up.

"One of your long days, I imagine?" Albert asked.

"No, not really. I stayed a little later in order to plan how to make tomorrow a little easier; easy is never how my days go. So what's on your mind?" Lebron said.

"Nothing that you won't be able to handle," Albert replied.

"Come in and lay your troubles on me," said Lebron.

"Hey honey!" Lebron shouted when he opened the house door. "I'm home and look who I found!"

"Have a seat Albert. Make yourself at home. Would you like a drink?" Lebron asked.

"Whatever you are having is fine for me," Albert replied.

"Hi honey," Lebrons' wife said when she entered the room. She greeted him with a kiss. "You're late!"

She then turned to Albert.

"How nice to see you again." She hugged him. "So what good news do you have for us?" she asked, taking a seat beside him.

"If you can describe what I am going to ask of you both as good news, then by all means it is good news. I have been thinking that it would be good to have a companion with me on my trip to Trombago. Mara and I discussed it and agreed that I could ask you if you both will allow Manzi to accompany me, that is if he would want to," said Albert.

"Well let's see what he thinks about that," said Lebron, and left the room to fetch Manzi.

"Hi Uncle Bert!" Manzi said when he entered the room.

"Hello Manzi, how are you?" Albert responded.

"I am fine sir," said Manzi.

"Your uncle wants to take you with him to his homeland

for a couple of weeks. What do you think?" said Lebron.

"Really? Really?" said Manzi excitedly.

Manzi bent over and hugged Albert tightly.

"Well there is your answer," said Lebron.

"When do you plan to leave?" Manzi asked.

"In about two weeks' time," said Albert.

"Not so fast young man," Lebron interjected. "When is your school closing for the holidays?"

"In three weeks," Manzi replied.

"Well we can have you excused for a week, but you are going to make up for it at home. You are going to make up that week you will miss by studying right here at home before you get to go anywhere," said Lebron.

"Yes dad, I will. You won't have to remind me," said Manzi.

"Now that we have that settled, you can go back to your homework," said Lebron.

"The fact that he will be travelling out of the country means that he will need international travel documents. You should be able to obtain a passport, or some equivalent travel authorization, from the government without any problems. With your influence I am sure that you can have that done in a very short time," said Albert.

"Don't worry about that," said Lebron. "I can get that done in less than a week."

"I will take care of his airline ticket and accommodations. He will be in very good and firm hands since he will be staying with my parents and I," said Albert.

"Thank you for thinking of him. I know that he looks up to you a great deal and even wishes to have a career similar to yours. This should be a very good experience for him, something he can use in the future," said Lebron.

"Think nothing of it. Remember you all gave me back my life in ways that you don't even realize. I am the one that is truly thankful," said Albert. "Well, let me head back home. Remember to take care of getting those travel documents for Manzi."

Martel greeted Albert when he opened the door of Maras' house.

"Daddy!" The little boy jumped into Alberts' outstretched arms. "Daddy, we ate dinner!"

"Did you leave some for me?" Albert asked him.

"Yes daddy!" Martel replied.

"Good boy," Albert said, and kissed him before putting him down.

"So how did it go?" Mara asked.

"As you had expected, they were all in agreement. Manzi was so excited," Albert replied. "So everything is settled, with only a few minor details to sort out."

56

News of rioting and violence in South America pervaded the airwaves. Riots had broken out in various parts of the country, with demonstrators accusing the government of corruption and of neglecting the needs of its citizens. The riots continued throughout the day and night, without much abatement, and many people were killed. Most recently the leader of the country and some key government officials were killed. At that point the death toll was three hundred and, until the riots subsided and a new leader was elected, army personnel began to run the country.

People all over the world who had relatives in South America became more and more concerned. Grant was no exception. He had tried for several days to contact Mary, but without success. A sense of calm was restored two days after the South American leader was pronounced dead and the army began to run the country, but small groups of demonstrators still rioted in the southern areas where the poorer people lived. Finally, Grant received a call from Mary.

"Hi dad. You must have been wondering whether anything happened to me. I am safe and well. The riots did not affect me or my team. As a matter of fact we were provided the best protection available, and never felt threatened in any way. The people here are very friendly, honest, and religious. They only ask to be treated fairly but, as usual, politics always gets in the way of that. I could say a lot more, but I would need private circumstances to do so," she said.

Grant, although relieved to hear from her, was still concerned about her safety.

"Why don't you come here until things return to

normal?" he asked. "I am sure that I don't have to mention how much we miss you."

"I am working on something here that is going to keep me busy for at least two weeks and furthermore all plane departures and arrivals have been restricted for another three weeks. But I promise you dad, I will be there as soon as possible," Mary said.

"That is one promise I am going to hold you to, as we are deeply concerned. Be very careful and remember that we miss and love you very much," said Grant.

"I love you too dad, so express my love to Jean and everyone there. See you all soon," said Mary.

Grant hung up the telephone and immediately called Wren.

"Hi Wren, how are you and the family keeping?" he asked him.

"Hi Dad! Everyone here is well and in good spirits! How is everyone on the island doing?" said Wren.

"As well as can be I must say. Mary is doing well too. I finally got in touch with her. She called me a little while ago and she is safe. She said that she and her team have been provided protection during the riots and they are not in danger," said Grant.

"I am so glad to hear that Mary is safe, as we were worried stiff after hearing about the uprisings. It would be good if she could get out of there until things go back to normal or, for that matter, get out of there for good," said Wren.

"She is not going to leave there until she has achieved the goals she has set. She is too dedicated to make failure become an issue. I suggested that she should come and stay with us for a while. She promised to be with us in a couple of weeks," said Grant. "While I am on the subject of her visit, why don't you and your family come here too and join us? We can make it into a family reunion."

"That is a good idea. Let me work on it," said Wren.

"Oh by the way, I got some news that maybe Albert is

alive. His father got a call from someone, presumably him. I believe that he will be coming to the island in a week or two. I don't know how this is going to affect Jean and I, but I am sure that we will be able to work it out," said Grant.

"Some time ago I read in the newspapers that the Agency Albert had worked for had arrested quite a number of government officials, executives, and land developers on various charges, including murder. They did not report a lot of details since the investigation was ongoing and most of the information was classified," said Wren.

"Really? Oh. I guess I will be hearing the details when this supposed Albert gets here," said Grant.

57

Now that the day of Alberts' departure to Trombago had finally arrived, Manzi was overcome with anxiety and a tremendous amount of anticipation. His sister Dori, although happy for him, was disappointed that she would not be going. While on the way to pick up Albert for the trip to the airport, Lebron assured her that he would take her and her mother to Trombago next year.

"Be on your best behavior. Be respectful to everyone that you encounter," Lebron admonished Manzi.

"I will dad," Manzi promised.

Once Lebron arrived, Albert hugged and kissed Mara and Martel.

"I will call you the minute the plane lands," Albert promised them.

"Hi there," Albert said, as he got into the car.

"Hello," Lebron and his children replied, almost in unison.

"All rearing to go?" Albert asked Manzi.

"Yes Uncle Bert," Manzi replied.

"He is very excited," said Lebron.

"Good," said Albert. "This experience will add so much to his character."

Manzi had never travelled farther than the immediate area surrounding the Reservation. As he sat in the airport terminal with Albert, he was bewildered. The terminal was busy – travelers were moving back and forth, flight arrivals, flight departures and boarding instructions were being announced over loudspeakers, and groups of people hung out in various restaurants and eateries.

Albert noticed his puzzled expression.

"What you are seeing is the difference between your

culture, environment and social activities, and that of the world-at-large. Your way of life is much different. It's more contained and restrained, with a leisurely undertone, less focus on business and industry, less technology, and a greater sense of control. The world at large is fast-paced, hectic and profit-driven. It is likely that many years from now, with young people from the Reservation like yourself and your sister becoming well educated, some of the things you learn about the world-at-large will be implemented to make life better for the people at the Reservation. Once that happens the Reservation may take on qualities similar to what you are seeing here."

The airline agent announced the boarding of their flight and Albert and Manzi joined the line of passengers entering the aircraft. A short time later they were airborne.

"How does the pilot know where to go?" Manzi asked.

"Well there is a flight path to travel by, and the pilot uses the instrument panel in many different ways to help him navigate," Albert replied.

Three hours later their aircraft landed in Trombago. Olan and Alicia were at the airport to meet them. When Albert saw them he dropped his bags and ran into their arms. Alicia was sobbing, overcome with joy at seeing her son alive and well.

"It's so good to see you son," she said. "Welcome home."

"Welcome home and happy birthday my son!" said Olan.

"Thank you both. It's so good to see you both," Albert replied.

Manzi and the luggage attendant slowly approached them with all the luggage.

"Mom, dad, meet Manzi. He played a major role in saving my life. I will tell you more about that later," said Albert.

"Glad to meet you son," said Olan. He and Alicia hugged Manzi.

"Come with us," said Olan. "We are parked close by and will be on our way in no time."

On the ride home Albert commented on the expanded roads and the many new homes that had been erected.

"The developments in the country over the years has helped all the citizens in many areas of their lives," Olan said.

"This is the house I grew up in," Albert said to Manzi when they arrived home.

"It reminds me of my own home in Malutica, only prettier," Manzi replied.

Alicia led them into the house.

"Manzi, you will occupy this room," she said, opening the door to a small room nestled at the back of the house. "Don't be afraid to use all the conveniences we have provided for you."

"Thank you ma'am, I will," Manzi replied.

Albert had already walked into his old bedroom.

"I see you have made a lot of changes," he said when his mother joined him. "Everything has a modern appearance, especially the new furniture and furnishings. And yet, the house still emits the same safety and comfort I experienced as a child."

Alicia nodded.

"I am glad you feel the comfort of home," she replied. "Your father is on the verandah. After unpacking you can join us there. In the meantime I will make some refreshments."

Albert finished unpacking and then helped Manzi to put his things in the right places. Soon they both joined Olan on the verandah. It was still early in the afternoon and Alicia treated them to freshly made sandwiches and lemonade.

Albert explained the details surrounding his trip to Malutica, the accident, his amnesia, and the necessary secrecy about his existence. He then credited Manzi with saving his life by taking him home to his father when he found him in a coma.

"Manzis' wonderful family and the kindhearted people on the Reservation helped me during my suffering and nurtured me to full recovery. I owe it to them, as well as to myself, to help make their lives better," said Albert.

"I was a bit skeptical when you called, as you were classified as dead and were even confirmed dead. You mentioned your concerns about locating Jean and Adrean but hung up before I could tell you that Jean is here on the island," Olan said.

"Really?" Albert said. He was surprised. "Here? In Trombago? Wow."

"There is a big issue facing you that both you and her will need to resolve though. It is best that you are aware of it before you see her," said Olan.

Olan took a sip of lemonade.

"I must tell you that Jean and Grant are married and are residing not very far from here," he continued. "I had informed them after you called that it is likely that you are still alive. This is something that you will all have to face and find the best resolution in a rational way."

"After regaining my memory I have been agonizing over the suffering and ordeal that she and Adrean might have been experiencing. It is consoling for me to now know that Grant was, and still is, there for her. My love and undying friendship for him has now grown stronger. In my heart this issue is already resolved. There is no blame or excuse for what we face. I too have been involved with someone else. While suffering from amnesia I fell in love with the nurse assigned to take care of me. We now have a son, so you have a grandson named Martel. Now that my memory is restored I realize that so many lives have been disrupted and so many complications have arisen. However, with understanding, and honest and sincere discussion and decisions, all these things can be resolved," said Albert. "It is still early. Can we go and see Jean and Grant now and then be back home in time for dinner?"

"Sure! Let me call them and let them know that we will be stopping by," said Olan.

When they arrived at Grants' house, both he and Jean came outdoors to greet them. Grant hugged Albert with the same degree of love and affection that they had shared all their lives. Jean was tearful and very nervous but hugged Albert firmly. She then ushered everyone inside, and held Alberts' hand on the way in.

Grant got busy preparing refreshments once everyone was seated inside. Albert looked around. He had been impressed by the beauty and aura of the exterior of the property and was equally impressed with the interior of the house. There was a warm and cozy feeling inside, and the layout was modern, bright and airy. The furniture and decorations were tasteful and elegant.

Soon Grant returned with a tray of crudité, crackers and an assortment of cheeses. He also brought freshly made fruit juice.

"We should be welcoming you with champagne, but this will have to do for now," he said with a smile.

"I am so thankful that I am alive to share not only a glass of juice, but this moment of renewed friendship, fond memories, and the unity of family," said Albert.

Alicia seized that moment to introduce Manzi as the newly accepted member of the family.

"This young man is in part responsible for saving Alberts' life," she said. "When we spoke with him we got a thorough understanding of the difficult time Albert has experienced. We are not only thankful for him, but forever grateful to him, his father and all the people of his homeland for the effort, sacrifice and contribution they all made to Alberts' recovery and well-being."

Albert shared the details of the ordeal he had undergone over the years. Grant sighed and shook his head in total commiseration. He held Jeans' hand as she failed to stifle a sob and tears rolled down her cheeks.

"It was several weeks after I regained my memory that my doctor finally approved my return to the city. I returned with a delegation of officials to help bring the criminals, who had committed murder and stolen land from the people of Malutica, to justice. These same criminals had implemented various methods to cheat Denham City residents out of their homes. My primary goal, however, was to find you and Adrean," Albert explained. "When I met with Nora and Blair as part of the group of officials, they had no knowledge that I was still alive. It took much effort to convince them that it was me. At the time my hair was long, and I had a beard and moustache, so it was difficult for them to recognize me. Once I shared details about the investigation that I had been involved in on behalf of the Agency however, and disclosed some classified information, they became convinced. Nora made some inquiries and then informed me that you had sold the house to an old friend. Eventually I met with your friend Ann and she told me that you and Adrean might be somewhere in Europe, since she believed that Adrean may be employed there, but she wasn't sure which country you were in. She is also concerned and would love to hear from you."

Albert sighed.

"Would it be alright to continue our discussion tomorrow? There is so much to talk about, so many things that have an impact on our lives and on which we will have to make decisions. Can you make yourself available Grant? I would love to have you present with Jean and I," he said.

"Sure, after one o'clock would be good for me. I can come and pick you up," said Grant.

"Well tomorrow you will have him all to yourselves, so let me take him and Manzi to a waiting dinner and some well-earned rest tonight," said Olan.

Jean and Grant walked the visitors outside to the car and, once more, Jean held Alberts' hand on the way.

"No one is to be blamed for the way things are with you and Grant. It is how I would want it to have been all these years," Albert assured her. "We will talk tomorrow."

He kissed her on the cheek.

Alicia had prepared a delicious meal for them, and they quickly and heartily consumed it while watching the news on the television. Soon, after dinner, Manzi began showing signs of weariness and retired for the night.

Albert and his parents stayed awake discussing his ordeal for a few more hours.

"I was so afraid when I first began to recall the day of the tragedy," said Albert. "I would get sporadic visions of the car I was in, the helicopter, and the trees. But the worst part was the sound of the gunshots. I would wake up in the night in a cold sweat. My doctor, Preston, was so very good. He gave me very small doses of medication to help me through my recovery."

"I am so glad it is all over now," Olan said.

"Me too," said Alicia. "My darling son. I am so glad that you are alive."

Alicia choked back some tears and sighed. Albert hugged and kissed her.

"I love you and dad so much. I am so glad to be here with you both," he said.

When they retired for the night their hearts were filled with the peace and joy that resulted from them being together again.

58

As promised, Grant came to pick up Albert at one o'clock. Albert was in a relaxed mood. Throughout the morning he had spent time in the garden helping his father tend the vegetables and fruits. Then he and Manzi had rummaged through his old toys and books. He was amazed that his parents had kept so many of them, and just as amazed that they were in good condition. Manzi was fascinated by the stories Albert shared about his childhood. When Albert departed for Grants' house he was absorbed in one of Alberts' old books, and Alberts' parents were preoccupied with their daily activities.

"You look extremely well and focused for someone who has gone through so much!" said Grant.

"I was lucky to have been found, cared for, loved, and inspired by some wonderful people during my difficulties. I have no doubt that you too would be impressed with the honesty, kindness and wisdom that the people of Malutica possess. I am still lucky to be a part of their community," said Albert.

"That is so good for you Albert. You are indeed fortunate," Grant replied.

On the way to his house Grant gave Albert a tour of the areas surrounding the town and slowed down at the places they had frequented as young men. The men felt the warmth and strength of the bond they had shared all their lives and chuckled at the memory of some of the childish antics they had gotten into as children.

When they arrived at Grants' house Jean was busy preparing lunch.

"Go ahead and be seated, lunch will be ready in a couple of minutes," she said. "Grant did you show Albert around the neighborhood?"

"I sure did and it is amazing how familiar he still is with some of the places we frequented as kids, despite the changes that have been made to them over the years," said Grant.

Soon the three of them ate lunch at the kitchen table situated directly in front of a big bay window. The sun was at its' peak but was not shining directly in through the window since the window faced east. Albert enjoyed the brightness that came through it nonetheless and marveled at the lush greenness of the beautifully manicured lawn. He felt happy that Jean had found such a paradise.

Lunch was delicious and after eating the three of them relocated to the sitting room, carrying glasses filled with wine.

"I was devastated when I heard of your tragedy," Jean explained. "Nora had come by the house with the news. She was very caring and consoling. A few days after she broke the news she provided me with some of your personal belongings and a death certificate. The hardest thing I had to live through was not having your body. I never imagined that I would see you alive after so many years."

"After many years of consoling each other Jean and I realized that we could support each other better if we were together, so we decided to get married," said Grant.

"Once I got to Trombago my parents made me aware that you had married each other. I was surprised, but not disappointed. The fact is that I would not want it any other way under the circumstances. You both felt the need to comfort and support each other when consolation was badly needed. It was an honorable thing to do. I respect your decision and admire you both for it. I have no reservations or remorse," said Albert. "In all fairness though, I have to admit that I am also involved in a relationship. It started while I was still suffering from amnesia. A nurse had been assigned to personally care for me and take care of my medical and therapeutic needs. Perhaps because of loneliness, or because of physical attraction, our connection developed into a loving relationship and now we have a son. We are not married but my love for her and my son, and for the people of Malutica, is growing stronger each day."

"Based on your evaluation and your honesty about your situation, I see where your approach is both rational and impartial. I also see that you now have a more practical and realistic view about things. It is a sign of someone that has developed a lot of humanitarian and spiritual traits. In my work as a doctor I have formed similar conclusions about others," said Grant.

"I think I see things in a realistic way, rather than in a speculative way. This does make me more at peace with myself," said Albert.

"I know that you have a lot of options," Jean remarked. "But what are your plans for the future? It is very important for us to know how your future will be affected by the decisions you make. The love that you and I share is very special, and I am sure that it will always remain in our hearts."

"Remember that you and I were not separated by disagreement, but because of reasons beyond our control. I can see the happiness and sincerity that you and Grant share and, as I said before, I accept and applaud the fact that you have made a successful life together. It is so obvious that you both have found your place, and I too have found mine," Albert said. "I desperately need to see Adrean though. I miss her terribly and there are a number of things that she should be made aware of. I can imagine the state of confusion she might be in, but I know that she is very strong and has a great sense of understanding."

"Adrean will be arriving here on Wednesday at noon, so you can rest assured that you will see her then. When we told her that you were going to be here, she immediately made arrangements to get here at the earliest date possible. We are not sure if Mary and Wren will join us here, but they both promised to make every effort to do so," Grant said.

"Seems like this is going to be a family reunion," said Albert. "I am looking forward to seeing everyone, but I regret that it has been so many years since I last saw everyone."

"Would you care to stay for dinner?" Jean asked. "I could fix something in no time."

"I would like to, but mom is making something special today and to disappoint her would be like asking to be scolded. Which reminds me, I should be getting back there soon. I love your home, the comfort it affords, and the hospitality you have extended. Not to mention, I love you both deeply," said Albert.

"Let me make a quick change and I will accompany you both back to your parents' house," said Jean.

"We will wait in the garden while you get ready," said Grant.

When Albert entered the garden, he was amazed. Even though he had enjoyed the vista from the bay window in the kitchen, he was delighted to explore the intricacies of the garden.

"Your garden is well cared for!" he remarked. "I am sure that you have contributed very little to its upkeep. You have never been one to like gardening."

"I do now," said Grant. "Jean and I both take care of the plants, but twice a week we have a professional come by and provide maintenance services."

"Well here I am!" Jean shouted from the house door. "I hope I did not keep you guys waiting too long!"

"Not at all," Albert replied. "We have been busy enjoying the beauty of your garden."

They arrived at Olans' house to find Alicia making the final preparations for dinner.

"Olan took Manzi to the store with him," she explained. "I expect them back any minute now. Make yourselves at home. I do hope that you will be staying for dinner."

Just then Olan returned.

"Hello, hello," he said. "It's good to see you guys here."

"Come with me Jean. I could use some help setting the table," said Alicia.

Soon Olan asked Albert to bless the table and he was very brief and effective in doing so. The group then enjoyed the scrumptious meal that Alicia had prepared. Being with his parents, best friend and Jean felt like old times to Albert.

On their way home Jean sighed.

"I am so pleased with the way the day went. Did you get a sense that Albert is now a religious person? For instance, the blessing he gave at dinner and the openness and acceptance he professed regarding our marriage; he actually absolved us. If you actually analyze it, what he really did was to make the decision for us all. I think that is so amazing," she said.

"I don't see him as completely religious. He is more of a spiritual person, which makes him appear divine. Spirituality does have religious underpinnings, but it all depends on the path one chooses to take," said Grant. "The day went well indeed. Albert and I will always be like brothers to each other."

59

On Wednesday Adrean arrived safely from Europe. When Grant and Jean picked her up at the airport she immediately asked to be taken to see her dad before going home to stay with them. When they arrived at Alicias' home Albert was busy tending to the fruit, herb and vegetable plants in the garden – a pastime he had grown to love while recovering at the Reservation in Malutica.

Adrean ran into his arms with tears in her eyes. They hugged each other and held on tightly, for what seemed like forever, before Albert let her go slightly.

"My beautiful daughter," he said, as he looked into her eyes. Ever so gently he wiped the tears from her cheeks and kissed each of them.

Albert and Adrean walked, hand in hand, to the verandah and sat down in the comfortable chairs there. Albert listened as Adrean shared the developments in her life over the years. He wanted to hear everything. He wanted to know her joys, her fears, her pain. He wanted to fill any void that existed since he had been missing from her life. There was so much to discuss, so much to know.

"I am so glad that we are reunited," he said to her. "And now that we are reunited we have more time than ever to catch up on everything. I will be here for another five weeks. While you are here, we will spend time together and enjoy the strong bond and love that we have always shared."

"How soon will we be together again? I want to hear how things have been for you over the past years," she said.

"Definitely tomorrow my dear, and every day until you leave Trombago," he replied, and hugged her.

Albert and Adrean optimized Adreans' three week vacation by spending several hours with each other daily. Adrean got a full understanding of the ordeal her father had undergone and the circumstances under which he had recovered and survived. Her understanding deepened her admiration of his strength, perseverance, resilience and courage.

During those three weeks more family members and friends arrived to share in the joy of Alberts' survival. Wren and his family arrived on the same plane with Nora, and Mary arrived the day after they did. Nora stayed at the Himda Resort while Wren and his family stayed with Mary, Grant and Jean.

A grand reunion at the Himda Resort was planned. Everyone was excited. All the visiting family and friends were anxious to see Albert and confirm that he was alive and well. They all were curious about what had happened during the many years that he had been missing from their lives.

When the day of the reunion finally arrived, Albert was ready. He knew that he would have to expend a lot of effort and energy to share his experiences and also give necessary attention and assurances to his many friends and family members. He decided to recount salient events from his experiences to the gathering at large. This was easier than repeating them to individuals or to smaller groups. He highlighted the more memorable moments and then Nora spoke about the day when she discovered that Albert was alive.

"Members of my staff and I met privately with a delegation from Malutica," she said. "I will skip most of the detail and get to the main point. There was a gentleman in the delegation who was standing by himself, to the side of the group. His hair was long, and he sported a beard and moustache. He looked somewhat like an Indian. While the other members in the delegation spoke at length, he said nothing. I asked the man leading the delegation who he was and whether he could speak. I was told that he could speak, and that he was the person that would make the criminal case we were working on indisputable. He then revealed that the man was Albert. I remember thinking, What the hell is he telling me? And then the man spoke for the first time and insisted that he was Albert. He described events and provided the secret codes we had used as team members at the Agency. Even though I still felt some disbelief, I knew that only Albert could have known about the events and the codes. I asked him a few more pointed questions and finally became convinced. It was at my request that Albert kept his identity hidden until our Agency had made necessary arrests, since our Agency felt that his life was still in danger. It so happens that we have someone here who played a pivotal role in saving his life. We will now ask Manzi to briefly tell us about this."

Manzi was shy but Alicia nudged him, and so he stood up and described how he had found Albert bleeding at the foot of a tree.

"My sister and I took him home to my father who immediately called the doctor. The doctor told us that he had suffered broken bones, lost much blood from the wound on his head, and was in a coma. We then moved him from our house to the house where the Chief of the Reservation lived. A nurse was assigned to take care of him there. When Uncle Bert came out of his coma, the doctor realized that he was suffering from amnesia. His amnesia lasted many years."

Once Manzi sat down, Olan stood up.

"Our family thanks all those who helped in Alberts' safety, healing, and recovery. Some of those people are here, and others are in Malutica."

He turned and spoke to Manzi.

"Young man, in appreciation of your unselfish and quick thinking actions we accept you as the newest member of our family."

"Thank you sir," Manzi said humbly.

"We are not quite finished," he said to Manzi. "I present these books to you on behalf of our family. One is a history of Trombago and the other is a history of the lives of the

Arawak Indians. Our family has also formed a foundation to assist four children from Malutica in their college pursuits. Although we have formed it here Nora has promised to have it fully supported when she returns to the United States."

Manzi rose and looked around at the gathering with humility.

"Thank you sir. Thank you on behalf of the people of Malutica," he said.

"Such a responsible young man," Jean whispered to Grant.

In the days immediately preceding his departure from Trombago Albert asked to be taken shopping and to have Manzi see the school that he and Grant attended as boys. Even though the school was closed for the summer, Albert enjoyed walking around the grounds and sharing memories of his childhood days with Manzi.

When the day of departure arrived, Albert promised that he would visit Trombago frequently. He and Manzi had enjoyed every moment of their time on the island and would remember the islands' beauty and peace, as well as the wonderful reception and family reunion.

60

Lebron and Dori were at the airport to meet Albert and Manzi when they arrived in the United States. Dori was anxious to hear everything about their trip, and Manzi happily told her about the wonderful island of Trombago and the many things he had experienced. It was clear to Lebron and Dori that Manzi had enjoyed himself immensely. By the time they arrived at Maras' house he had fallen asleep.

Mara was sitting on the porch when they arrived. She and Albert hugged and kissed each other with affection. While Manzi and Dori took Alberts' luggage into the house, Mara and Albert chatted with Lebron.

"Thank you so much for allowing Manzi to come with me," Albert said. "He had such a good time. My family has adopted him."

Lebron smiled.

"I am proud of my son. I am glad that he had the opportunity to travel to a foreign country. Thank you my friend. We will visit you again soon."

Lebron departed for home and Mara and Albert hugged each other once more.

"So how was your trip?" she asked. "I missed you so much."

Albert rubbed his sons' head. Martel had been clinging to his arm and playing with his shirt collar.

"I missed you too, in so many ways," Albert said. "There is so much to tell you. It will take me the rest of the day. But overall I had a very fulfilling trip and I accomplished more than I had expected to."

"Did your parents recognize you? And what was their reaction?" Mara asked.

"They did in fact recognize me and they were overjoyed,

especially my mom who shed tears of joy," Albert replied.

"I was surprised on the day I arrived when they informed me that my wife was living on the island, and that she was married to my childhood best friend Grant. She and I met several times during my stay and we discussed various issues that we were concerned about. Grant was also present when we met. I disclosed that I am in a relationship from which I fathered a son. She admitted that she still had that special place in her heart for me. I shared that my love for her is still the same, but that I respected and sincerely honored the life that she had chosen with my best friend," said Albert. "Well, how have things been here since I've been gone? And son, have you been a good boy and taking care of mommy?"

"Yes daddy," Martel replied.

"Good boy," Albert said and rubbed his head once more.

"Things have been the same since you left. Lebron stopped by to see us often and, as usual, Choca is here every day," said Mara.

"Good old dependable!" Albert exclaimed. "How is he doing?"

"He is as good as can be, but he misses your company quite a lot," Mara replied.

"I am looking forward to seeing him soon. What are you making for dinner? I'm starving!" Albert said.

"I'm making baked chicken with vegetables and potatoes. It should be ready in less than thirty minutes," Mara replied.

"Good. I will take a shower in the meantime," said Albert.

Soon they were at the table eating dinner.

"Wow, you are really starving! I have never seen you eat so much!" Mara exclaimed.

"It is your cooking that I really missed," said Albert.

"Well, let me finish up here in the kitchen so that I can have my shower and be relaxed like you are," said Mara.

"You go ahead and take your shower," said Albert.

"Martel and I will tidy up and do the dishes. Right son?"

"Yes daddy," Martel replied.

"Oh no," Mara said. "You must be tired from travelling. Plus you are going to take all night. You and Martel can go and unpack."

Albert smiled. Mara always felt that he took a long time to finish any kind of housework. He decided not to challenge her about that. Instead he and Martel went to unpack.

"Here son, this is for you," said Albert, as he pulled a small box from his suitcase. "It is from your grandmother."

"Who is she daddy?" Martel asked.

"She is my mother," Albert replied.

"What is it?" Martel asked.

"It is a necklace. Her photograph is inside the pendant," Albert said. He opened the small pendant. "See? This is what she looks like. She wants you to keep this forever."

At that moment Mara joined them.

"Hold out your hand," Albert said to her.

When she did so, Albert placed a bracelet around her wrist.

"This is from me to you," he said to her. "And these plaques and photo album are from my parents."

"What are your parents like?" Mara asked.

"My father is from Scotland. He is very kind and considerate. My mother is from the island and is of African and English descent. She is loving, smart and sweet," said Albert.

"I can just imagine how happy they were to see you and to know that you are still alive," Mara commented.

"Everyone was overjoyed and expressed their joy in so many different ways," said Albert.

"It is now getting late. We should retire for the night," said Mara.

"Good idea. I long to be in your embrace, and badly need to enjoy our lovemaking," said Albert.

Martel had fallen asleep on the carpet and Albert tucked

him in his bed for the night before joining Mara in their bedroom. Their lovemaking was tender and passionate. They both were happy to be reunited after being apart for almost two months.

The following morning Albert and Mara were, as in the past, awakened by the chirping of the bird that frequented their garden.

"Has he been here chirping every day while I was away?" Albert asked.

"He has only shown up a couple of times," said Mara.

Albert got up, walked over to the window, and looked out into the garden.

"I see that he has now found a mate."

"I think he knows that you are back and wants to introduce his mate to you, and maybe also tell you something," said Mara.

"Now what could he possibly have to tell me?" said Albert.

"That I am going to have another baby," Mara replied.

"You are kidding me!" Albert exclaimed.

"No. It is true. I'm really pregnant," said Mara.

"So how in the hell would he know that? Are you sure our Mr. Bird is not the father?" said Albert.

"I'm sure. I have to admit though that he is some kind of guardian angel to be always hanging around us," Mara replied.

"We can get all the answers from Choca when he gets here. He is spiritually wise, and studies nature all the time," said Mara.

They didn't have to wait very long as Choca arrived a few minutes later.

"Welcome back my friend!" he said to Albert. "I sure missed you."

"You are not the only one," said Albert. "Our friend, the bird, did too. And he has now brought his mate along with him. I firmly believe that bird is watching over us."

221

"In a sense you are right," said Choca. "As long as you keep providing for him, he will always be here. The corn and the peas, the rich soil that produces worms, and the morning dew that provides water for birds to drink – these things will always attract them. You are a source of their existence, and they know it. As long as you keep providing, they will always appear."

"Well, come on in. Breakfast will be ready soon," said Albert.

Martel ran up to the door when he heard Chocas' voice.

"Look grandpa! Look what I draw!" he exclaimed while extending his drawing pad.

"Who is this, your daddy?" asked Choca.

"No grandpa! It's you!" said Martel.

Albert and Choca looked at each other and smiled.

"Who taught you to draw?" Choca asked.

"Nobody, I like to draw," said Martel.

"Keep at it son. One day you will be a famous artist," Choca remarked.

"Yes grandpa!" Martel exclaimed happily and ran off to find his mom.

"He is such a sweet boy," Choca said. "You must be so proud of him."

"I sure am," said Albert, "and I am proud of his mother too."

"Come on you guys, breakfast is ready," Mara called to them from the dining room.

She did not have to call them a second time. They were at the table in a flash. After breakfast they gathered on the porch and Albert related the events from his trip to Trombago. At one point he went inside and returned with a package for Choca.

"This is for you my friend," he said. "Go ahead and open it."

Choca opened the package and found a pipe and some tobacco neatly packed inside a wooden box.

"The pipe is custom made, and the tobacco is home

grown. My island home is known for growing the best tobacco in the world," said Albert.

"Thank you Bert," said Choca. "Maybe I should go ahead and sample it right now."

However, Choca smiled with satisfaction, closed the box, and placed it on his lap.

"Now you my friend are the first to know my intentions," said Albert. "I could never find a better time and occasion to ask Mara to marry me."

Mara blushed. Albert held her hand in his.

"I am not going to take no for an answer. Will you marry me?" he said to her.

Mara held back her tears.

"You know I will. Yes, I will," she replied.

They hugged and kissed.

"So this is what the bracelet was about," Mara murmured.

"You really did find your way," Choca commented, "and now you have truly found your place."

61

F our months after Albert proposed, he and Mara were married. He had ensured that his marriage to Jean was annulled and had made travel arrangements for his parents to attend the wedding in Malutica.

The wedding was a small affair, with his parents, Grant, Myrna, friends from the Agency, and friends and associates from the community in attendance. There was none of the normal fanfare typical of wedding receptions. Instead their reception was a quiet and elegant three course dinner at a small restaurant outside the Reservation, with a pianist playing smooth jazz.

Alberts' parents had wondered why he chose to live in Malutica when there were better locations and opportunities elsewhere. Once they got first-hand exposure to the people of Malutica and experienced their warmth, love and kindness, they were reminded of the comfort and love they shared in their community in Trombago. They were also encouraged by the prospects of future economic and cultural developments in Malutica, and by the desire that the people had to advance their conditions and circumstances. They realized that Malutica reminded them of conditions in Trombago many years ago – their island home that they had seen grow and become more prosperous over the years. They were encouraged by thoughts of similar growth and prosperity in Malutica in the years to come.

Alberts' parents were delighted to see Manzi once more, and to discover that he had excelled in school. During their visit they developed a close relationship with his parents and invited them to visit Trombago. Lebron quickly accepted the invitation and asked them if traveling back with them would be too early. Alicia and Olan were thrilled to have

Lebron and his family travel back to Trombago with them. Albert chuckled when he realized just how minor his parents' pleasure was, compared to the joy that Dori and her mother felt about travelling to Trombago.

62

Shortly after Albert and Mara were married, the accused and arrested perpetrators of corruption against Malutica and Denham City residents were tried in courts and most of them were found guilty on all counts. Sentencing for the Chief of Police was delayed for over six months, but he was eventually given four life sentences without parole for the deaths of Torch, Nelson, Manny, and the police officer whom he had shot in the back. His two accomplices were each sentenced to twenty-five years in prison for conspiracy in the murders of Manny and Nelson. Jimray Burns and some of his superiors were each sentenced to thirty-five years in prison for arson, the illegal acquisition of properties, and conspiracy in the murder of Torch. Flek was given a sentence of ten years for providing information that led to the deaths of Manny and Nelson. All properties illegally obtained in Malutica and Denham City were rightfully reinstated.

Malutica was now granted official government representation, and several new agencies were established to oversee operations in the area and ensure that those operations were legally authorized and performed. Lebron was elected mayor of the town and Norm, who had relocated to Malutica a few months earlier, was appointed to Lebrons' prior position. Aston was promoted to head the Housing and Employment department, and Keith was promoted to head a newly formed Education Ministry. The finance department was run by Douglas, a trusted financial advisor who had succeeded in obtaining resources which had been promised to Malutica as a result of its' exposure from the trials and the prosecution of the various public officials.

Government funds were now released to Malutica and,

along with revenue generated from the recovery of minerals from the hills, Malutica was expanding with the development of new well-constructed homes, properly engineered roads, and the installation of water and electric infrastructure.

Albert was asked to serve as legal administrator and accepted under the condition that he was authorized to institute some of his plans for Malutica. These plans included the institution of legal services, community awareness and entitlement provisions, as well as the conduct of scheduled town meetings to provide residents with updates on the strategies, methods and standards being deployed by all agencies and the progress of any development initiatives. Alberts' plans also included bi-weekly educational forums and lectures, and the dissemination of printed material on various topics useful in helping residents to make progress in various areas of their lives. His goal was to help residents develop trust in the government systems and programs being implemented, and to inspire them to be confident in their ability to realize their true potential.

Four children received funding for their college education within the first year of the program established as a result of the foundation formed by Alicia and Olan, and Manzi was one of them. Manzi is now in college and is hoping to be a lawyer. Dori is working hard to be selected for a scholarship next year.

Malutica is now a growing and prosperous city, thanks to the honest and dedicated people who, with love and kindness, made it their place.

With two boys, a loving wife, and a newly acquired home, Albert had really found his place, and a place had found him.

ABOUT THE AUTHOR

Fren Thompson was born and raised in Jamaica, West Indies, and is the fifth and youngest offspring of low-income parents. He grew up in a modest home where sharing was caring, giving was receiving, and being kind to others was being kind to yourself. Fren continued these practices throughout his life thereby exemplifying selflessness, sacrifice, and love.

Made in the USA
Columbia, SC
06 April 2021